GW01081062

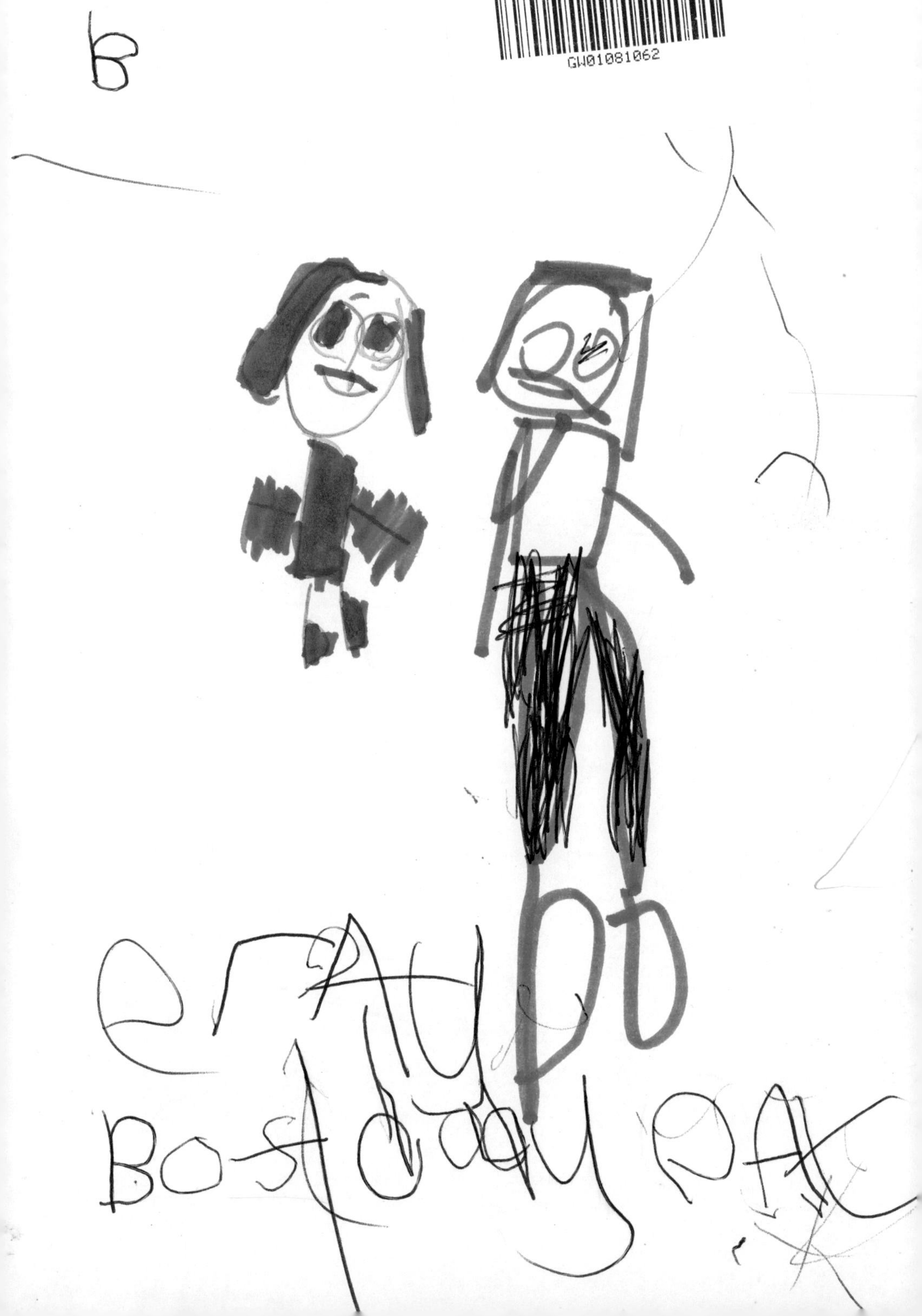

To ALL the Little Children in IBIZA

Best Wishes
Tony C.
IBZ 09

The Gnomes of Genom

by
Tony Curtis

authorHOUSE®

AuthorHouse™ UK Ltd.
500 Avebury Boulevard
Central Milton Keynes, MK9 2BE
www.authorhouse.co.uk
Phone: 08001974150

First published by AuthorHouse 2/23/2009

ISBN: 978-1-4389-5789-0

Printed in the United States of America
Bloomington, Indiana

This book is printed on acid-free paper.

This book is dedicated to my daughter Rachael, and to all parents who have lost a child through illness.

Rachael was an inspiring person, who had the ability to help others.

Also dedicated to my son, who is learning about life, day by day, also to my Grandson, Zach.

Contents

The Star of Life

I was a little bit lonely at first, wondering where I was, when two large hands came towards me and manhandled me into some sort of shopping trolley full of colourful plants and shrubs, which I'd never seen before. What on earth was happening? I seemed to be pushed around in the trolley for ages. Then, I heard this ringing sound as I was lifted from one trolley to another along with all the other things.

Outside in the bright sunlight, I was moved again into the back of a small black car and put on the window shelf along with some of the plants. The boot of the car was already full of boxes and plastic bags.

I could see through the window as we drove off, and I noticed a large green sign. We'd just left "Graham's Garden Centre". But who were these people? Where were they taking me? What was my fate to be?

Travelling along, I had a good view of everything, especially the cars behind us. While poking my head out from amongst the plants, I saw the people in these cars smiling at me and waving as we travelled along the country roads. I must have looked very funny.

As we approached a village, I noticed a lot of signs at the side of the road.

The largest sign written in large black letters on a white background said,

Genom Village Welcomes Safe Drivers

Please drive carefully.

All the other signs – there must have been at least twenty – were bright orange and said something about a beautiful gardens competition to be held in July.

Then, I fell asleep. I'd had a busy time, wondering what was going on.

I woke up to find myself sitting in the hazy sunshine at the bottom of someone's garden, near a little pond, which was overgrown with bushes. Tall trees cast long shadows over the stream beyond.

There was nobody around, even the people who brought me here. It was very quiet, except for the birds chattering to each other from tree to tree.

Suddenly, the wind started whistling all around me. It was an eerie sound. It made the hairs on the back of my neck quiver. I stayed very still not daring to move.

A man appeared from a large house in the distance wearing, what was compared to mine, very dull clothes. I liked my bright orange shirt, large red hat that protected me from the sun, and very blue trousers. He was dressed in a dark-grey shirt and trousers held up by a black belt. They were obviously his gardening clothes, because his trousers were covered in grassy stains, with the odd hole here and there.

The man walked slowly towards me, stopped, and looked all around, especially at the few fish in the pond.

I felt a bit uneasy and wondered if he'd seen me. I *do* stand out, dressed as I am.

He stood there as tall as I'd ever seen anything in my whole life – a giant compared to little me.

I realised that he *must* have seen me before, and I didn't seem to bother him. He just kept looking at me and smiling.

Then, someone else arrived from the side of the house. He was pushing a large green wheelbarrow full of earth, and he shouted, "Mr Temperton, where would you like me to put all this?"

Mr Temperton pointed and said, "Just over here, Jack, would be fine."

Jack,who is a close friend of Mr Temperton, and has worked for him for many years, made his way along the path, pushing the heavy wheelbarrow. He stumbled once or twice over the cracks in the path, and some of the earth spilled onto the path. He stopped to catch his breath. It must have been hard work pushing that heavy thing all the way from the house.

Then, he went into the garden shed and came out with a long-handled spade and a concrete sign. I didn't quite understand that. Jack slowly pushed his spade into the earth and sprinkled it all around the side of the pond.

He grabbed me by my head, which had me shaking with fear, and pushed my feet firmly into the new, soft soil.

"Little gnome," he told me, "this is your new home. We expect you to do a good job. Please take care and guard the garden, especially the fish in the pond. You look after us, and we'll look after you."

All of a sudden, Mr Temperton gave out a roar of laughter, as he read the sign that came from the garden shed.

"What are you laughing at?" asked Jack.

"I've just thought of a name for our little gnome," Mr

9

Temperton replied, still giggling.

"What do you mean?" Jack asked.

"Well, this sign that we bought this morning along with the gnome says,

"EVERY GNOME MUST HAVE A HOME".

"Yes?" said Jack, quizzing Mr Temperton.

"Must have a gnome! Got it?"

"Not really," snorted Jack.

"We'll call our little friend Mustafa! Mustafa Gnome!"

Jack burst out laughing. "That's very good. I wouldn't've thought of that one."

Hearing all this made me feel very important. I straightened my back and pulled my stomach in, standing as proud as I could.

"I am Mustafa."

Mr Temperton and Jack were in the garden all day, moving rocks, stones, and plants from my corner of the garden. And there they found, hidden beneath all the old grass cuttings, fallen twigs and moss, some statues. They were rather like me but with no colour, just an old-looking grey colour. There were tall ones, small ones, rabbit shapes, frogs, and what looked like a tortoise.

They looked at each other and started laughing again.

Mrs Temperton came out of the back door carrying a tray with three mugs of tea and a sugar bowl.

"Come on you two; I think you deserve a rest." She put the tray on a wooden table surrounded by a bench, which was tucked away in one of the other corners of the garden and shaded by a beautiful green, leafy tree.

"It sounds as if you two are enjoying yourselves," she said with a smile.

"We are, my dear," replied Mr Temperton, "and I think we are going to enjoy this garden much more than you can imagine."

As they sat and drank their tea, Mr Temperton started

referring to me as Mustafa, and, of course, Mrs Temperton had to be told how I came to be given my name.

After the story was told, Mr Temperton said, "We'll just have this drink, and then if I cut the grass, will you do the edges, Jack? Then, I think we'll call it a day. There's no point in trying to do it all at once."

It was strange to remember that only a few hours ago I was a lonely little gnome with nothing happening. Now there was so much activity in this garden: the fish in the pond, the wind gusting through the trees, the birds speaking to each other, sometimes frogs leaping about, and flies hovering over the pond and landing on the plants, which seemed to float on the surface.

I realised that I must have been specially chosen to guard all of Mr and Mrs Temperton's things. That made me feel very good. This nice couple would speak to me, every time they passed, to see if I was all right. They didn't know that I could think for myself, but I was quite happy in my own little world, without a care, just doing my job.

It was a big responsibility, although I just sat and watched, not like a scarecrow, whose job is to scare the birds away from the farmers' crops. We wanted our birds. I could see bags of seeds hanging off one of the trees to entice them into the garden.

Yes, I was a lonely gnome, wondering what the future held.

Now I was secure. I was needed. I had a new home.

It was beginning to get dark, and, oh, it was my first night. *Come on Mustafa, take a grip. You're not afraid of the dark.*

I was not on my own for long. Mr and Mrs Temperton came out of the house all dressed up and looking very smart and pushed a kind of machine onto the lawn. They put it down right in the middle. Jack followed carrying different coloured tables and chairs. Mrs Temperton went back in and came back with two large trays full of plates, knives and forks, lots of glasses, and a few bottles.

Mr Temperton started messing about with this little machine; it seemed to take ages, but it gave me something to watch and kept me occupied. I wondered what was going to happen?

Now Mr Temperton was putting on an apron! Oh dear me, he looks just like Mrs Temperton, except for the trousers.

Everything seemed peaceful enough. Did I dare close my eyes for a few moments? It had been a long day. "No, I should be on guard," I say to myself.

Suddenly, people started arriving from every angle, over the fence, by the side of the house, and through the back door. Where were they all coming from?

Some were carrying glasses, some parcels of meat, and a few had bottles.

Now there was rather a lot of noise, with music in the background I couldn't understand all the kissing and shaking of hands.

Then, Mr Temperton walked up to the machine on the lawn and pulled out this little box from his apron pocket. I squirmed with fear, to think that he could just make a light from a little piece of wood, point it at the machine, and everything just seemed to glow a bright red colour. But it was rather nice when I got used to it. It lit up my whole little world. The glow of this machine made me warm. I felt secure and happy. I was not alone anymore.

I was so tired by what had gone on during my first day in the Temperton's garden that I nearly fell asleep, when a huge flash streamed up into the moonlit sky.

I felt a kind of shudder, I shook, I felt sick, and I was scared. My little hat had turned bright green. I noticed that the statues in the corner had been affected by this happening too. The gnomes had some colour in their cheeks, and their clothes had turned the same colour as mine. The rabbit, frog, and tortoise appeared to have a new lease of life.

No one else seemed scared. They were all looking at

the coloured lights and saying "Ooooh!" and "Aaaah!" So, it must be all right.

I felt different. I felt warm inside. I felt loved. I felt great.

I was not tired any more. I felt ready for anything.

A spark from the barbecue must have hit a very remote star that can't be seen by the human naked eye.

That spark brought my tiny world to a beginning.

Gnomemansland had arrived!

The gnomes of Genom were sure to have some stories to tell.

The gnomes of Genom were here to stay!

Mustafa Meets His Friends

Remember me? My name's Mustafa. I'm the one who was in Mr and Mrs Temperton's garden the night they had a barbecue with lots of neighbours and something strange happened.

A flash of light came out of the barbecue and shot straight into the sky. It hit a remote star, which I've called the Star of Life, because it opened up my little world.

When the flash of light came, my clothes turned a different colour. My hat used to be red, but now it's green, and I was all alone at the bottom of the garden.

Now it's the day after the barbecue, and Jack and Mr Temperton are starting to clear up all the mess that's been left. There are glasses and plates everywhere. The plates must have been made of paper and have blown all over the place. Some have even got stuck in the hedge, and many more are hiding in the flowerbeds. It took them quite a long time to pick up everything and put it into a large plastic bag.

Mr Temperton slowly came to my corner of the garden, where they'd left me the day before. He stared at me and called Jack, "Jack, am I imagining things? Didn't Mustafa have a red hat last night, or did I enjoy myself too much?"

"Yes, you're right," Jack said. "It *was* a red hat. Either someone's playing a joke on us or something very funny is going on."

"LOOK!" said Mr Temperton, pointing to the pile of grass cuttings where they had found all the other grey statues. "All these other ones have green hats and bright clothes too. Something very peculiar is going on."

What they didn't know, and at that moment neither did I, was that the spark and the star joined together all their strength to spread happiness to all the garden ornaments in the village, bringing them partially to life in their own little way.

I looked in the corner to see what had changed, and, yes, I could see that many of the grey stone little faces had a pink tinge to them, colour in their eyes, and were dressed the same as me – except for the rabbit, frog, and tortoise. They're animals of course and take on a different colour to us gnomes. Anyway, they don't wear clothes.

Jack and Mr Temperton started to stand my friends up, as they looked uncomfortable lying on their sides. They arranged them in a group and then vanished back into the house.

Dare I speak to my new friends, I wondered? Will they understand me?

I swallowed and took a deep breath.

"Excuse me, but can you hear me?" I said in a very quiet voice.

"Of course we can, Mustafa," came the reply.

"How did you know my name?" I asked gingerly.

"Well we know; we're gnomes. We're old and weary,

and we've been in this garden for quite some time, just dumped and left by the couple who owned the large house before that nice Mr Temperton came along."

Another gnome spoke, "We were listening to everything that happened since you arrived."

"Last night we started feeling warm," the first one went on. "And suddenly our old grey clothes came to life."

"It must have been because we were laid on our side, and we haven't been able to talk to each other, ever since we arrived," came a weak little voice. "We saw you arrive, and we hoped that you might change things around here."

"Anyway my name's Sam, and this is my sister Ella. Don't ask me how we got our names; all I know is that we used to be at the farm at the other end of the village. I was perched on one tower of stones, and Ella was on another about six feet away, guarding the entrance to the sheep pen."

"Well it's nice to meet you," I said happily. "Let's hope

we don't get separated. I think Mr Temperton likes you. I think he might find you a job in his garden."

Suddenly, the stone rabbit rose from the pile of grass and hopped off along the steppingstones that led to the stream. I shouted after him, but he was gone.

"Oh leave him," said Ella. "He's always wanted to be free to explore this side of the village. He was with us at the farm, squatting near the cowshed, but he was scared of the big animals, especially when they started licking their lips. He always thought they wanted to eat him, but all they really wanted to do was smell him and lick his coat. He'll be back. We call him Raymond. Ray for short. Ray the Rover."

"Have you been in this village long?" I asked.

"Well long enough to know what goes on. We used to have red hats, and all the other gnomes had the same, but now I think we must be related, as we're dressed the same as you," Sam said. "They must have used the same mould."

"We seem to have a lot in common, certainly, but can we really be related?" I enquired.

With all our chatter, we didn't notice Jack walking back down the garden with a small brush. He took hold of Sam and started brushing him down. I could see a smile on his face. It must have been tickling him. Putting him to one side, he then took hold of Ella and did the same to her.

Walking past me, he entered the garden shed, came out with a bright plastic mushroom, placed it on the corner of the lawn, and put the twins side by side, just under the lip of the top. They looked as if they were sharing an umbrella, sheltering from the rain.

Jack turned around, picked up two more gnomes from the pile, and did the same to them. I haven't spoken to these two yet, but I was determined to find out where they came from and what their names were.

I hoped that he was not going to take them away. We seemed to have made friends. Well, after all, they could be my cousins.

Things were getting better all the time as I saw Ray hopping behind me along the bank of the stream. The twins said he'd come back, but he just kept on going. He checked out the neighbour's garden on the other side. I'm going to have to keep an eye on that one.

Mrs Temperton looked out of a window and shouted, "Jack, your lunch is ready!"

Jack put down his brush after brushing the soil off his shoes and headed back towards the house.

The garden was silent once more. Then suddenly, from the grass cuttings, came a deep groan.

"Oh it's nice to stand up again and stretch my legs," said a gruff voice.

"Hello, my name is Mustafa. What's yours?"

"Lofty. And you can tell why," came the reply.

He was the tallest gnome I had ever seen; he was thin, with a very red face and astrognomic arms, which stretched halfway down his legs. It must be because he was pushing a wheelbarrow.

"Oh, I'm tired of being attached to this thing," he said. "I must have been stuck to it for umpteen years; it's beginning to make my back hurt as well."

"I can't help you there," I said. "It's one of those things."

"I'd just like to be able to scratch my nose now and again, especially when a fly or insect lands on my face, but it's impossible because of this heavy wheelbarrow. Anyway, that's my problem, and I've grown to accept it."

"I must say that you do look great in that pose." I tried to cheer him up. "I should think Mr Temperton or Jack would put you right in the middle of the lawn where everybody could see you."

I heard another sound from the pile of grass cuttings.

"I hope there isn't a pond or stream nearby," came a very light-hearted voice.

Looking across, I saw another gnome with a green

hat, hanging onto a fishing rod. I started laughing, and he joined in. We both found it very funny.

"I'm sorry. We've this little pond and that stream just at the bottom down there," I told him.

"I don't have a name, but if everyone else has one, I'm sure somebody will give me one. I'm the fishing gnome, and I always find myself by a pond watching my own reflection in the water. Never get bored or tired, I just sit and watch the fish swimming around," he continued. "They feel safe with me around."

Ray hopped back into the garden through a hole in the fence, which separated our garden from the one next door, and went up to Sam and Ella.

"It's not raining is it?" he said to the twins, as they stood under the mushroom, smiling at him.

"Oh you're back," said Sam. "I knew you would be. You wouldn't leave us two on our own."

"There are green hats everywhere," said Ray, gasping

for breath, "and I've only been two or three doors away."

"Really? That's amazing! What a difference that spark has made to our world," I said. "We must contact all the green hats that we can and have a meeting to introduce ourselves and find out more about what's been going on in this sleepy little village."

Jack came out of the house with a mug of tea and walked towards us.

Ray hopped back into the grass cuttings along with Lofty and the fisherman, and they tried to cover themselves. I can't think why. Jack's a nice sort of man and wouldn't hurt them.

Jack picked up the brush, got hold of Lofty, gave him a good brushing down, and walked to the middle of the lawn. A small smile came over my face. "Told you so," I whispered.

Lofty turned to me and just grinned.

He looked like a picture, standing proudly right in the

centre of the freshly cut lawn, pushing his wheelbarrow.

Jack said, "I think we'll put some plants in your barrow tomorrow, young man."

Hee, hee! Lofty is here for good.

For the rest of the day, it was only Jack in the garden, pottering around, clearing weeds from the flower borders, walking in and out of the shed, and picking up leaves that had fallen from the trees.

He walked back to the shed, emerged with the same brush that he had used on Lofty, picked up the fisherman, and placed him at the side of the pond.

This time, it was the fisherman who turned to me, with that sort of glance that said, "I told you so."

The clouds were building up in the sky; it looked very overcast. We might end up with some rain later. It would be nice to have some rain. It's been very hot and humid over the last few days. It would brighten up the colours in the garden by giving the flowers, plants, and lawn a well-deserved drink. It'll make the air fresher too.

A few seconds later, I felt some drops on the top of my head. Jack put all his tools away and ran into the house.

This was an ideal time to get to know all my new friends properly and to find out from Raymond where he went and whom he met. I hoped he didn't say anything to any of them. We, the gnomes of Genom in the Temperton's garden, had to talk things over first and make plans for the future.

Raymond Has Done His Job

The sky was getting more overcast over the Temperton's garden. The clouds were joining together and swirling around in the evening sky making everything seem dull and grey. This was an ideal time to try and get to know the new friends I met during the day and to find out more about Raymond the rabbit's travels around this part of the village.

I felt more and more drops of rain falling around me, and it looked as though the clouds were going to open up and spread their load of water all over the village.

"What a lucky couple," I said to myself, as I watched Sam and Ella huddle together under the plastic mushroom. "That should keep them nice and dry as the rain slowly runs down the side of the large dome shape."

"Come on everyone. There's no one around. Let's have a get together and a little chat," I shouted.

Lofty shouted back, "That's a good idea, Mustafa. I've only been in this garden one day. My arms are beginning to hurt after holding this barrow all day. I could do with a rest."

The fisherman gnome motioned with his rod and said, "Why don't we get out of the rain and shelter with the twins under the mushroom? I get splashed when it rains, because I'm sitting so close to the pond."

"Good idea," Raymond yawned, tired after his journey.

Within seconds, we were all under the mushroom. The fisherman started laughing. Lofty was too tall and had to crawl on his hands and knees to get some shelter.

"It's not fair, being tall, is it Lofty?" sniggered the fisherman.

"It does have some drawbacks, but at least I don't have to wear rubber wellies all day, looking at myself in the reflection from the pond," Lofty retorted.

The two shook hands. It was their way of welcoming

each other.

"I'm going to call you Jester," Lofty said. "You always seem to be joking, and nothing much bothers you."

"Oh, it does, but I never moan because nobody wants to listen, and I'm always placed well away from you other gnomes, but now I have a name. Thanks Lofty."

"Right, come on everybody. We all know each other. Let's find out what Raymond knows from his little break this afternoon," I said, trying to bring them all to order.

We all finally got under the mushroom, as the rain became heavier.

"Get on with it Ray," Ella said. "We haven't got all day."

Raymond yawned again, but you could feel the excitement, because he knew he had everyone's attention.

"I just don't know where to start," he said quickly.

"Try the beginning; that's the normal place to start," Jester quipped.

"Well, something really fascinating has happened to this side of the village. I didn't go too far in case I got lost, but in every garden I visited, all the gnomes had green hats just like your's. All were nicely dressed, with rosy red cheeks and very pleasant to talk to. They don't know what happened the other night either. There was one gnome who was dressed slightly different to the rest. I mean, he had a skirt on and what looked like a sponge on his head and a very well-tailored beard. His voice was a little bit different. I found it hard to understand what he was saying. I understood his name though. It was Willy."

"Well gang, what shall we do?" I asked. "I suggest that we invite one gnome from every garden to come here and meet us."

"Before we do that, we ought to give our group a name," Lofty mumbled.

"OK, who are we?"

"We are the gnomes of Genom, and we live in Gnomemansland," Lofty replied, this time in a very strong voice.

"Ho! Ho! You're right on the ball!" Jester laughed.

The rain started to ease off to just a few drops here and there, although it was still running off the mushroom dome.

"OK. If there aren't any more suggestions, I propose that we sleep on the idea and discuss it tomorrow. I'm very tired, and I feel as though I've run halfway round a racecourse," yawned Ray, his eyes nearly closed.

They all started making their way back to their positions – Jester by the pond, Lofty in the middle of the lawn, and me standing guard, with Sam and Ella still under the mushroom.

Night fell quickly. The sky was very dark, and everything had gone quiet. Even the lights in the big house had gone off. It was time to have a sleep.

After a while, Lofty stirred and opened one eye as he heard footsteps.

"Mustafa are you awake?" he whispered.

"I am now!" I whispered back.

"We have visitors. D'you know who they are?" Lofty said with a shudder in his voice.

"No. Be on your guard. I don't know what they're doing here."

The others heard Lofty and me and began to wake up, listening to what was going on.

A great burst of light illuminated the garden. It was very bright, which made the gnomes blink. This light was attached to the outside of the big house. It must have come on when the sensors detected the movement of the two visitors.

When we stopped blinking, we could see two people dressed all in black, with dark hats over their faces. They look startled as the light cast their shadows all the way down the garden. They began to run away from the house towards Lofty. I could see that the tall gnome knew exactly what to do.

He moved his wheelbarrow slowly towards the two people, who now had their heads down and were running as fast as they could.

Whoops! Oh, dear! Wallop! One had tripped over the barrow and fell flat on his face. He got up in a sort of daze and carried on towards the stream at the bottom of the garden.

"Ouch! Ooh! That hurt!" someone shouted.

One of them was coming close to Jester, who realised he had to act. He turned quickly and flicked his fishing line towards the oncoming intruder. It wrapped itself round his ankles and tripped him up. He was flat on the ground trussed up like a turkey.

The one behind hauled him to his feet, and they scampered off towards the stream and jumped over the fence into the garden next door.

"Well done everybody," I shouted in a firm voice, feeling

very proud of my friends.

"Ooh! That hurt!" came a feeble voice from somewhere in the darkness as the lights on the house went out.

"It's Timmy!" yelped Sam.

"Who's Timmy?" we all asked.

"He's the tortoise who was in the grass cuttings with us," called Ella.

"Something stood on me. Ooh! It still hurts!" cried Timmy.

"What were you doing over there anyway?" Lofty asked.

"I was on my way to the meeting and got lost," said Timmy sadly. "I'm a slow old fool you know, and then it got dark; so, I thought the best thing to do was stay where I was until it got light, but I fell asleep. When the lights came on, I found I was in the middle of the lawn, not far away from Lofty."

"Well, you certainly slowed down those two runners

and gave Jester enough time to cast his line around the ankles of one," I praised him.

"Hey! My fishing line has broken, and I've lost my little red float off the end. I hope I won't get into trouble," joked Jester.

"If Mr Temperton knew what went on here tonight, I doubt if he'd mind a broken fishing line," I told him. "Now, let's all get some sleep. It's been an interesting night for all of us."

The Meeting of the Clan

The sun slowly began to rise, spreading its light all over the Temperton's garden.

From where I was standing, I could hear all the others chattering away about what went on last night with the two burglars, Lofty and his wheelbarrow, Timmy the tortoise being stood on, and poor old Jester, the fisherman gnome, losing his fishing line.

Time passes by so quickly when you have things to keep you occupied. We've had lots to talk about.

Ray the rabbit came up to me and asked if he could go and tell all the other friends he has made from the other gardens about us.

"I'd wait until we have the meeting, Ray. You could go and mention that we'll meet in the early evening when Jack and Mr Temperton have their tea," I said firmly.

It pleased me to know that my friends looked on me as

their leader – the one who has to make the decisions.

"OK, Mustafa," Raymond said, and hopped off into the distance.

I think he feels wanted. He's got a purpose, because he knows he's the only way that we can get messages to all the gnomes in the other gardens, and, of course, he's met them all before.

The sun was getting very warm now. The shadows from the trees were getting smaller. The flies and insects began their daily routine of hovering around the flowers, having a good smell, and then travelling onto the next one.

Lofty emerged from his slumbers and realised that his wheelbarrow was still in the middle of the lawn, with the contents sprayed all over the grass.

"This isn't right," he called.

"We can't do anything about it Lofty. We'll have to rely on Jack to sort it out – that and my broken fishing line," Jester said in a tired voice.

Voices were coming from the house and getting louder and louder.

"It's a lovely day," shouted Mr Temperton, as he walked out of the back door. "Come on, Jack. Let's get to work and get this garden up to scratch. It's not long now to the competition."

Mr Temperton walked round to the front of the house, whilst Jack emerged from the back door.

He stopped. He noticed a plant pot that was just under the kitchen window. It must have been knocked over last night. He stooped, picked it up, put it on the window sill, went back into the house, and came out with a small brush to sweep the path.

Walking onto the lawn, he noticed Lofty's wheelbarrow lying on its side. He stopped again and scratched his head. Mr Temperton joined him, carrying a large pot, which he was moving from the front of the house to the back.

Jack turned to him. "Something's happened again, Mr

Temperton. That plant pot on the window sill was on the floor, and the wheelbarrow's fallen over. I don't remember hearing anything during the night, do you?"

"Not a thing," replied Mr Temperton. "Never mind. You were going to put some new flowers in the wheelbarrow today anyway weren't you?"

"Yes, that's my first job, and then I thought I'd concentrate on that corner and try to tidy it up."

"Oh dear!" whispered Timmy. "He's going to find out that my shell is cracked."

"Don't worry about your shell, what about me?" snorted Jester.

Jack started working in the other corner of the garden and went into the shed, just as Ray hopped back down the garden.

"Everything's arranged," he shouted. "One gnome from each garden will be here tonight about teatime."

"Hey Jester!" shouted Ray, "I think I've seen your fishing

line and float."

"Where?" Jester asked excitedly.

"Down by the edge of the stream, tangled on some branches. I would have got it for you, but the branch overhangs the water, and if I bounced on it, I would have fallen in the stream."

"Come on! Let's go! Show me where it is," said Jester running off.

"Wait! Can we help?" asked the twins, Sam and Ella, as they appeared from under the mushroom and started running after Jester.

At the stream, they stood and wondered how they could reach the line. It was quite high up on the branch.

"Pass me that stick over there," shouted Ella. "Now hold onto my arm Sam."

She reached up and had to lean over the edge of the water with Sam holding onto her other arm, as she tried to reach and release the line.

"Oh, it's in a really awkward position and well and truly wrapped round the branch," she said stretching as far as she could.

"Let me try. I'm used to hanging onto a rod. I should be able to reach it," Jester said.

They changed places. Jester took the stick. Sam held onto Jester. Ray held onto Sam, while Ella shouted out the instructions. Jester leaned out as far as he dared, holding the stick as high as he could.

"It's coming! It's coming!" he shouted.

Only two seconds later, Jester slipped. Snap! Splash! He ended up in the stream. Luckily for him, it was not very deep, but the water was high enough to flow into his wellies.

"Oh no! I had it! It's floating down the stream now," he laughed.

"Quickly Ray! Hop off after it, and see where it ends up," shouted Sam.

Raymond was off like a rocket, while Jester tried to walk through the stream in the same direction. It was obviously not easy for him. His wellies were full of water.

Struggle! Splash! Poor Jester was flat on his back as he slipped again, on a stone this time. He just layed there, laughing as usual, with the water lapping slowly around him.

"Why don't we just forget it," laughed Jester.

"All right, we will," came an excited voice from behind a bush. "I've got it!" Ray looked very proud of himself.

"Oh thank heavens," said Jester. "I've got no energy left. I need to dry off, so let's go back and see what the rest are doing."

Poor Jack and Mr Temperton had worked very hard all day digging up weeds, moving plants, and giving them lots of water to drink, while Mrs Temperton had been washing all the clothes and hanging them out to dry.

The sun was going down when Jester and his friends

arrived back in the garden. They were just in time to see all the other gnomes arriving for the meeting.

They all talked and shook hands in the friendliest manner until I called the meeting to order.

"Friends, my name's Mustafa. I'm the gnome responsible for all the new, exciting things that have been happening around here. I didn't know it had affected other gardens in the area, until Raymond, our friendly rabbit – Ray for short – came back the other day with the news that all of you have been given a new lease of life. So, welcome. I think the best way to start is if we all sit round in a circle and introduce ourselves by giving our names and saying which garden you each come from and anything else that might interest us all."

"OK, I'll start. It looks as though I'm one of the oldest here." This was the voice of the gnome wearing the skirt and sponge on his head. "My name's Willy. I'm from a country called Scotland. I moved down here a few months ago with Mr and Mrs McCue who live at No 40. There are only four gnomes in our garden, and they're all dressed like me."

"Nice to meet you Willy. We're pleased to have you on our side," I told him.

The next one to speak was a gnome called Jim, who was sitting to the right of Willy.

"I'm from two doors away, and there are only two of us. It's nice to meet new friends."

They all introduced themselves in turn. There was Willy, Jim, Button, Plank, Sugar, and Simon. They reported that there were at least sixteen other gnomes apart from us.

I thanked them all for coming, and I told them how the spark from the barbecue hit the Star of Life and brought us all together.

"If it's all right with all of you, I propose that we call ourselves "The Gnomes of Genom" and form our own clan. Sorry about the pun, Willy," I apologised.

"Och, don't worry about that, Mustafa, laddie," Willy

replied. "We're pleased you arrived when you did," he added with a warm smile on his face.

"What's going to happen next?" asked Button – aptly named since he only had one button left on his coat.

"Well," I thought for a moment, "we ought to find out more about the village and how many more ornaments there are out there that have been affected like we have. I'm sure we'll meet again, but if you want to wander around the village and you come across something of importance, will you please let me know? I know for sure that Raymond the rover rabbit wants to travel about. Anyway, we have the garden competition to look forward to. I think Mr and Mrs Temperton are going to enter, and I am sure many of you will be there as well. We all know now that we can move about at night, so please be careful. Only yesterday my friends here, especially Lofty, Timmy and Jester, helped stop two burglars getting into the big house over there," I cautioned them. "We all have to work together, so let's try and make this a safe village."

"One thing that we could do to start with," said Plank, "is to pick up the litter in the streets when we move around. Nobody will see us, and it would be a worthwhile task."

"If we're going to work together, that's a good job to start with," chirped Simon, who was a little bit slow in talking and very quietly spoken.

Willy stood up. "OK, laddies, let's get to work, and don't forget to be on your guard."

Fun in the Park

Evening had arrived in the sleepy village of Genom. All the gnomes were determined to carry out the promises that they made at the meeting held during the day in the garden where Mustafa and his friends met for the first time after the amazing spark from a little barbecue in Mr and Mrs Temperton's garden changed their lives forever.

All the garden representatives returned to their friends after the meeting in high spirits. They all wanted to try and impress all their newfound fellow members of the clan known as the Gnomes of Genom.

They all agreed to try and keep the village safe and clean by picking up all the little bits of litter that suddenly appeared on the paths and in the gardens of the residents and most certainly keeping their eyes open in case anything unusual happened.

Most of the residents in the village and surrounding farms were preparing for the summer garden competition by painting fences, planting flowers, and cutting their lawns.

After the sun had gone down, Jester, the funny fisherman, and Raymond, the rabbit, decided to go and wander around the village. Jester, who always spent the day sitting by a stream or a pond, wanted to expand his knowledge of the area. Raymond was the only one who had gone hopping about, firstly to find all the other gnomes and ornaments in the surrounding gardens and secondly to tell them about the meeting where they all introduced themselves. So Jester knew that Raymond knew his way around and was the ideal choice to go with him.

"OK Jester, where do you want to start?" Ray whispered.

"I would have thought the best place is the far end of the village, so that we can slowly make our way home, and, hopefully, by doing it that way, we won't get lost."

"Clever thinking my funny friend," Raymond said. "Let's go and explore."

They quietly left Mr and Mrs Temperton's garden, because they didn't want to wake any of their friends, who by this time were all fast asleep after another long and busy day.

After squeezing between the railings of the double gates at the front of the house, which brought them onto a footpath dimly lit by the street lights, they spotted a dark shadow, which seemed to be coming from the hedge.

"Where do you two think you're going?" came a little voice out of the shadow.

"Who's there?" Raymond whispered.

"It's me, Plank. I met you at the meeting."

"Oh yes," replied Jester, "but what are you doing out here?"

"I decided that I should try and be the first to check out the village, just to see how much work will be involved in trying to keep this place tidy."

"By the way, why are you called Plank? It's a bit of a silly name," Jester sniggered.

"As you can see, I'm taller than average, slim, and have a flat face. All my friends say that I always misunderstand what's being said, so I'm thick, hence the name Plank."

"That figures," Raymond laughed. "Do you want to join us? We're going to the far end of the village and then making our way back here."

"If that's all right. I think I'd be scared on my own," Plank smiled, feeling a little better for being with someone.

It took them 15 minutes. They followed the main street through the sleepy village, where they ended up not far away from a large building, with a sign outside that said

"Green End Farm".

"I think we've gone far enough now. Let's turn back," Plank said, shivering with cold and fear.

"I remember this place; I used to live here with Sam

and his sister Ella. I thought it was further away than this. I'll have to come back sometime to investigate a little more. Anyway, you're right. We should turn around and head back to where we came from. It's a straight road, so we can't get lost," Raymond whispered.

On the return journey, they decided not to talk so much, so that they could concentrate on the houses and buildings that they passed and so that they would be able to report to all the other gnomes in the morning.

"Good gosh, that's a big building!" Plank screamed, standing back in amazement. "I wonder what that's for."

It looked like a very big house. There was plenty of land at the front with a few cars parked on it, green plants growing up the front over the arched front door, and a large sign that seemed to spread right across the building that said "Genom Green Hotel".

Plank turned to Jester and Raymond and asked, "What's a hotel?"

"I've seen one before. It's where people come and stay for a few nights when they are away from home. They have a bedroom and can eat and drink," Jester said smugly.

"Oh, it's a gnome from home! Plank laughed.

Raymond indicated with his arm saying, "Come on you two; let's carry on."

Striding out, they passed a post office, a village shop, a news agency, and a gift shop before they noticed a small park on their right-hand side. They entered very carefully, as they hadn't come across anything like this before.

Plank and Jester were amazed to see so many different-sized frames with things hanging off them, a large object with steps up one side, and a few round objects that seemed to rotate in the light breeze.

"What do you make of this?" Jester shouted, as he ran towards one of the round objects. He grabbed hold of it and jumped on. As soon as he did, it started going round a little bit faster. "Weeeh! I like this," he smiled.

"Those are called roundabouts. That big thing over there with the steps on it is a slide. You climb up the steps, sit down, and slide all the way to the bottom. It's good fun. Those hanging things are known as swings. You just sit on them and rock backwards and forwards, but you must hold on, otherwise you could fall off and hurt yourself," Raymond said, in a know-it-all voice.

"Hey, this could be fun. Why don't we go and get some of the others?" Plank shouted.

"If you wake them up at this time of night, they're going to blame *me*. I know I joke a lot, but this is taking it a bit too far. Anyway, Willie is past this sort of thing, although it's right up Simple Simon's street. Let's leave it for another time," Jester said, yawning. "We'll call it a night, as we don't know what tomorrow will bring."

They stayed in the park for five more minutes, having a last go on all the rides before heading back home.

Up the slight hill in the centre of the village, they came across a litter bin that had blown over in the wind. It wasn't full, but some of the sweet papers that the children in the village had put in the bin had fallen out; so, Raymond and Plank did the job of picking them up and standing the bin in the proper place out of the wind.

Turning to Plank, Raymond said, "Goodnight. We'll see you sometime tomorrow. Have a good rest."

Firmly back in their surroundings, Jester and Raymond felt that they had achieved something worthwhile tonight, which brought a pleasant glow to their faces and lots of satisfaction.

Daylight broke, and Jester was seated by the pond with his rod held firmly in his hand and a smug grin on his face as the morning sunlight just caught the roundness of his cheeks. He was back in command of his own situation, whilst Raymond was still asleep. All that hopping around last night had taken it out of him. He would need another day to get over it.

In the neighbour's garden, Plank was just waking up. "I feel great this morning," he said to his friends. "I went out last night, paired up with Jester and Raymond from next door, and we explored the village. It was great." He continued with his story all through the morning.

Mr Temperton and Jack were out early this morning, as the competition was getting closer and closer everyday. They both had wellingtons on with thick socks, and their trousers were tucked in at the top. They looked set for a long day as they pushed a green wheelbarrow with a big spade, fork, and a rake laid on the top. They were heading straight for the centre of a flower bed on the left-hand side of the garden.

"What time's the new tree arriving?" Mr Temperton asked.

"I think the garden centre said about half past ten to eleven, depending on what other deliveries they have in the area," Jack replied, as he started walking backwards towards the shed. "All we have to do is start digging the hole, and they'll plant the new tree, because it could be quite heavy. Then we can sort out the rest of the plants to go round it."

He turned sharply and knocked poor old Lofty and his wheelbarrow over, spilling all the contents over the lawn.

"Oh no! Look what you've done," snarled Mr Temperton angrily, noticing that Lofty had broken his arm.

"I'm ever so sorry. I wasn't looking where I was going," Jack replied. "I should be able to mend it in time for the competition."

Slowly bending down, he picked Lofty up off the grass and carefully carried him into the garden shed. Jack placed him on the wooden bench next to some potted plants, while Mr Temperton tried to clean up all the soil that had fallen out of the wheelbarrow with a stiff brush and a spade.

"I think the plants will be all right," Mr Temperton shouted. "Will you be able to do anything with the broken gnome?"

"I'm just going to mix a little bit of concrete and stick

the arm back on and wrap a wet rag round it so that it doesn't dry too quickly, otherwise it might fall off again," Jack replied.

Mustafa, Sam and Ella, and all their friends could hear everything that was going on and felt so sorry for Lofty. They hoped he'd be all right. By this time, Raymond had stirred from his slumber and promised to go and see Lofty when things had quieted down.

"Good morning. How are things today?" came a gruff voice from the corner of the house. "I've got a tree that wants planting. Where do you want us to put it?"

"Just over here. We've only just started digging the hole, because we didn't really know what time you were coming," Mr Temperton shouted.

"I'm a little bit early. I have a lot of deliveries this morning, and, as usual, everybody wants things doing yesterday. I've only got one pair of hands," shouted the man in a gruff, sturdy voice.

He turned and went back to his lorry where two more men had started getting the tree onto some sort of trolley so that they could push it to the back garden and put it in position.

Jack came rushing out of the shed, picked up a spade, and started digging as Mr Temperton walked to the front to see if the men needed a hand.

Timmy the tortoise couldn't believe his eyes and wondered what all the rushing about was for. His motto was always more haste less speed.

The three men emerged with the trolley and the tree, and they had no problem planting it, as by this time, Jack had made a large hole.

They got the tree in the ground swiftly, and the man who seemed to be in charge asked, "Which way would you like it to face?" Standing back and walking round the garden whilst looking at the new addition, Mr Temperton said, "That position is just perfect. You can see its shape from every angle."

"Would any of you like a cup of tea?" Mrs Temperton shouted from the kitchen window.

"No thanks. We've nearly finished," replied the smallest of the three men.

With that, they picked up their tools and the trolley and headed back to their lorry.

"Cheerio, Mr Temperton. I hope we'll see you again soon," said the man with the gruff voice.

"Cheerio and thank you," Mr Temperton replied.

"That's a nice-looking tree. Colourful, as well," Jack remarked.

"It's a pomegranate tree. It's quite old and just beginning to flower, but we'll have to be careful, as when the fruit drops, it can make such a mess on the ground. So, we must remember to pick the fruit at the right time." Mr Temperton smiled. "Are you ready for that cup of tea, Jack?"

"I think I'll just stick the arm back on this gnome first," Jack replied, as he walked back into the shed. "I won't be too long."

Mr Temperton went into the house and returned two minutes later with two mugs of tea – one for Jack, and one for himself – and sat down on the wooden bench just near the back door.

Meanwhile, Jack left the shed with a contented grin on his face and headed towards Timmy, carrying a small bowl. He bent down and started putting a small bit of cement onto Timmy's cracked shell, saying, "I don't know what's happened to you, but let's get it sorted now, whilst the cement is still soft."

After returning the bowl to the shed, he went and sat on the same bench as Mr Temperton to have his tea.

"It feels as though we've done a day's work already, and it's only ten o'clock," Jack said in a tired voice.

"I've got an appointment with the bank manager at twelve, and he's taking me out for lunch, so I'll have to get cleaned up before I go. I'll have to leave the rest to you

Jack, if that's alright," Mr Temperton said, as he sipped his tea.

"Well, all I'm going to do today now is finish painting the shed. I should have done it weeks ago," Jack replied.

For the rest of the day, Jack painted the shed and checked on Lofty every hour to see if he was on the mend. At about half past three, he decided to call it a day and returned inside for another cup of tea and a shower to clean himself up.

Sam and Ella along with Raymond now had their chance to go and see if Lofty was all right.

"How are you doing Lofty?" Ella whispered, as Sam tried to rub paint off his jacket, which got caught on the door on the way in.

"Not too bad. It was just an accident, but that man named Jack acted very quickly; so within a couple of days, a rub down and a bit of paint I should be ready to go back in the garden," Lofty sighed, with a few tears in his eyes.

"That's good news, but if you want anything, just give us a shout. We're only across the garden," Sam said, putting his jacket back on.

"I know. You're good friends, but you will have to take my turn in watching the back of the house," Lofty replied.

Raymond, Sam, and his sister turned to go out of the door and said, "Lofty, what are friends for?"

Party Time

Mr Temperton arrived back from his lunch with the bank manager carrying a briefcase. He left it by the back door and took a stroll around the garden, checking to see what Jack had been doing. He looked into the shed to see if he had been able to fix the arm back onto the gnome that usually stood in the centre of the lawn holding a wheelbarrow. The gnome's arm had accidentally got broken this morning just before the pomegranate tree was delivered. He was pleased with what he saw: Lofty standing on the bench with both arms attached and a bandage over the broken one. The shed had been painted with a new coat of brown paint and looked just like a new one. He then headed inside the house and picked up the briefcase on the way.

Willy, the Scottish gnome who lived in the garden of Mr and Mrs McCue at Number 40, popped his head over the fence and laughed when he saw Mustafa sitting and talking with Sam, Ella, Timmy the tortoise, and Jester around the pond.

"I've been looking for you in the wrong garden," he laughed. "I thought it was funny when I bumped into Plank. Oh, he can talk when he wants to! He hasn't stopped talking all day about his adventure last night. I do admit, it sounds fun. The park, I mean, with all the rides and everything. We should all try it tonight. Let's have a party."

Mustafa looked at Willy, who had now climbed through the fence, followed by his four friends, who were all dressed the same as Willy with those silly sponges on their heads and in brightly coloured skirts.

"I've just heard the same story from Jester, and I agree it does sound fun, but we must be careful," Mustafa said. "Are these your friends who come from the same garden?"

"Aye Laddie," Willy remarked in his Scottish voice. "This is Jimmy, Johnny, Jamie, and Justin. We've been together a very long time."

"Nice to meet you at last," Jester sniggered, "but you do really look funny dressed like that."

"We could say the same about you. You forget that we're from Scotland. It's the national dress up there," Jimmy reminded him. "We tend to speak with a strong accent as well."

"Have you heard about poor old Lofty at your part of the village," Timmy asked in a slow, drooling voice.

"No, what has he gone and done now? Nothing silly I hope," Willy asked quizzingly.

"He accidentally got knocked over this morning and broke his arm. They've stuck it back on, but it'll take a couple of days before he's back to his normal self," Ella said.

"When you see him, give him my regards, and I hope he'll be back on his feet soon," Willy said, turning to Ella. "Anyway, are we going to have this party tonight? Raymond can go and tell all the other gnomes. He's the fastest, and he knows his way round."

"If you like," Mustafa said, thinking deeply, "but we still have our jobs to do. We're not here to enjoy ourselves, and we can't afford anything to interfere with our objective. I'll get Raymond to go round and tell them about the park and that if they want to meet at the entrance gate when all the lights in the nearby houses have gone out, that's all right, but everybody has to be very quiet."

Jester and Mustafa went off to find Raymond and gave him his instructions, while Willy and his friends popped their heads round the garden shed door to speak to Lofty, before they returned to their own garden, using the same route as they had on their way in. A deep silence hung over the gardens, with the smell of anticipation in the air. The Gnomes of Genom couldn't wait for the party to start.

Darkness fell, house lights flickered on and off for what seemed like hours, until at last everything became quiet.

Button, Plank, and Simon were the first to arrive at the

gate. Plank couldn't wait to try the slide. He didn't dare try it last night, because it looked so huge in the dim light, but tonight he was determined to have a go. Leaning against the fence, Button and Simon waited patiently for the rest to arrive.

They didn't have to wait for long before they saw Willy, Jimmy, and Justin dancing down the street holding hands.

"I thought there were five of you. There were this morning," Plank said.

"Aye, Laddie, there are, but Johnny and Jamie aren't the party types. They take things very seriously and were prepared to stay in the garden," Willy whispered breathlessly.

Sam, Ella, Jester, Raymond, and Mustafa arrived shortly after.

"Are we all here?" Mustafa asked.

"I told everybody, but I didn't say it was compulsory, so a few might turn up later. Let's get cracking. I can't wait,"

Raymond said excitedly.

"Off you go, then, but as I said before, be very careful. We don't want anymore accidents. I'll wait a few minutes for Timmy and any more who turn up," Mustafa said.

They all dashed off as fast as they could to see who would be the first onto the roundabout, which was already turning slowly in the night air.

"Come on you slow coaches," Raymond shouted, who was the first to get there. "There's enough room for all of us on here." With one leg on the roundabout, he pushed it round with his other leg, making it go faster and faster.

"Hold on a minute," Ella shouted. "I can't get on; it's going too fast. Can you slow it down a bit?"

With that, Sam put a foot down, scraping the ground, which slowed the ride down, so that his sister could climb on.

"Wahay, this is different! I've never done this before; it's making me go dizzy!" Jimmy squealed.

"Oh shut up," Justin snarled. "You always complain. Just sit back and enjoy it."

"He's right. It's making me feel sick as well. Can we make it go slower?" shouted Plank, panicking.

"I'll stop it, so you can get off if you like, and then you can go and try the swings or the slide; otherwise, we'll all have to start queuing 'cos there are only four swings," Raymond said, putting both feet on the ground.

The roundabout stopped. Ella, Jimmy, and Plank jumped off, just as Mustafa and Button arrived to take their places.

"We're going to the swings now," Ella shouted. Then, she ran off, followed by the other two.

"Where's Timmy?" asked Jester, shouting into Mustafa's ear.

"I don't know. He hasn't turned up yet," Mustafa replied.

Sitting on one of the swings, Ella turned to Plank and

said, "I'm missing Lofty now. He could have stood behind and gave me a push. His long arms would have been handy, because I can't get this thing to move very well."

"I'm tall; let me try for you," Plank replied.

He positioned himself behind Ella's swing and pushed with one hand, which turned her round and made her crash into the swing next to her.

"Plank, you've got it wrong again!" Ella screamed. "Use two hands."

"That's better, but not too hard. Don't scare her," Jimmy shouted. "Can you do the same for me?"

Plank was now just standing there, pushing one and then the other, feeling proud. Meanwhile, some of the others had made their way to the slide, taking turns to stand at the bottom and catching each other as they hurtled towards the ground. Willy had been the first down and had slid right off the end, fell over, and hurt himself.

Willy walked round the back of the slide and noticed

something shining in the distance, just near the park's fence. He strolled over to it, bent down, and picked it up, looking puzzled. Suddenly, he jumped backwards in horror, dropping it onto the grass. Picking it up again, very slowly, he looked right in the middle of it, and said, "Who are you and what are you doing here?"

He received no reply from the image. He turned in a hurry and called out to Raymond, "Come here quickly! There's a funny-looking person staring at me from this piece of shiny rock. He won't say anything. He just moves his mouth."

"Let me have a look," Raymond said, pushing Willy out of the way.

Raymond turned to Willy, held his hand over his mouth, and tried not to burst into laughter. "That funny-looking person is you," he snorted. "It's your reflection. Everything you see is an exact copy of yourself. Everything you do or every movement you make, you can watch it at the same time. It's called a mirror," Raymond said in a voice of authority.

"Well you learn something everyday, don't you?" Willy laughed. He looked at himself, swayed his head from side to side, and checked himself out while he smiled, frowned, and even stuck his tongue out at himself. "Oh, I like this!" he said. "Can I take it back to the garden?"

"I would suggest not. Mr and Mrs Temperton, like all the people who live in houses, have mirrors like this one on their walls, and if they found a broken one in the garden, they'd wonder where it came from. They're not the sort of things that just turn up at the bottom of your garden," Raymond told him.

"You're right as usual. I'll leave it here, hidden under this pile of grass cuttings, but don't tell anyone. It'll be our secret," Willy whispered.

Walking away from their little secret, they heard another cry for help. This time it was Sam, who was with his sister. Sam was sitting on a large piece of wood, with one end up in the air. He was on the end that was resting on the ground, with Ella trying to push the other end down.

"What am I supposed to do with this?" Ella cried.

"You need to climb and sit on this end. Then, you'll be able to go up and down, with one on each end. It's called a see-saw. You just push up and down. Many of the children I've seen using this sort of ride sing a little song, as they do it," Raymond told them. "Look, I'll show you."

Raymond asked Sam to stretch his legs a little so that the see-saw would come down. Ray climbed on, and they both started rocking up and down.

"Hey, this is good," Sam said, looking at Ella.

"Get off Raymond, and let me have a go," Ella said excitedly.

Raymond hopped off, and Sam's end dropped sharply to the ground with a thump.

"Ooh, I didn't expect that!" Sam said, rubbing his bottom. "Be careful getting on Ella."

The twins were nicely balanced, going up and down.

However, Sam got the hang of it and started pushing harder with his legs until Ella, who wasn't holding on properly, fell off into the sand below.

"You're too strong for me. I've had enough," Ella complained, limping to the edge of the sand pit. "Find someone else."

Walking back towards the swings, she saw Jimmy and Justin hanging from a climbing frame. They could climb, swing upside down, and twist in and out of the frame.

"You look as though you have to be strong for that one," Ella shouted to Justin.

"You have. It's not for little girls," Justin replied.

Suddenly, Mustafa's voice echoed round the park. "Come on everyone. It's time we started heading back home."

"Do we have to? We're really enjoying ourselves," Raymond grumbled.

"Yes I think we do. It's getting late, and I'm getting

worried, because Timmy hasn't even turned up. You know he set off when we did. I wonder what's happened to him," Mustafa said in a firm voice.

All the Gnomes of Genom made their way to the park gate and said goodbye to each other and headed for home.

Button and Willy stopped suddenly. Willy saw something sparkling on the footpath in the moonlight.

"I think it's another mirror," Willy remarked.

"What's a mirror?" Button asked, walking quicker.

Thinking he might let his secret out, Willy said, "Oh you won't understand," grabbing Button by his coat.

"Watch out, you'll pull my last button off if you're not careful," Button screamed.

"I'm sorry. Look! I think it's Timmy," Willy shouted.

They both rushed across the road to greet him.

"You're a bit late," Button said, bending over to speak to

Timmy. "We're all heading back now. It's getting late."

"It's taken me ages to get here. The paths aren't as flat as I thought, and many have those little cracks that make it harder for me to get over. If you're all going home, I think I'll stay here for a few minutes to get my breath back and follow on later," Timmy whispered in a very tired voice.

"Will you be all right on your own?" Willy asked with concern.

"I should think so. I'm usually on my own because I'm so slow, but it's not my fault. I'll only be a minute. Then I'll follow you," Timmy said. He turned and crossed the road very carefully and entered the gate to the park, where he met all the others. "I know I'm late, but never mind. You get off, and I'll see you all in the morning," Timmy gasped, still trying to catch his breath.

Everyone left. Timmy was all alone once more.

"Why turn around and head back now," he thought to himself. "I might as well have a look at what I've missed."

He crawled towards the roundabout but couldn't understand what it was for. He looked at the swings and then the slide. He said to himself, "I'm too slow and too old for this sort of thing, and these things are far bigger than I thought. It's not for me. I'll just have a rest and start on my journey."

Poor old Timmy was exhausted and fell asleep, curling his head back into his little shell.

Willy, Jimmy, and Justin arrived back home to find that somebody had taken the gates off the hinges. They began to feel embarrassed that they had been out enjoying themselves, leaving Johnny all alone. Trust something like this to happen. They knew deep down in the back of their minds that they had failed in their duties to Mr and Mrs McCue and to all their fellow gnomes. They had failed to keep their promise to guard the village against such things.

"Johnny are you all right?" Jimmy shouted, running into the back garden.

"Of course I am; did you have a good time?" Johnny asked.

"Yes we did; it was very exciting, and we learnt quite a lot from the other gnomes. You could say it was a GASTROGNOMIC night, but we noticed that someone has taken the gates off. They're just laid up against the hedge," Willy said with concern.

"I did hear something, but it didn't alarm me. I'm sure it was Mr McCue's voice," Johnny said.

"Oh well, we might have got it wrong. We'll have to wait until the morning to see what's happening."

Meanwhile, Timmy had been asleep for quite a long time. He awoke, looked out of his shell, and noticed that it was still dark but not as dark as before. "Daylight isn't far away," he thought to himself. "I'd better start making my way home."

He left the park and crossed the road again. He knew that if he followed the same route, he shouldn't get lost.

Travelling along at his usual steady pace, he noticed a man walking backwards and forwards through the front gardens with some sort of metal carrier bag that was full of white bottles. The man, who was dressed in a long white coat with a hat to match, jumped into his car, which had no doors on it, and moved slowly down the road. He stopped, pulled out a small book with a pencil attached, and started making notes. Timmy was alongside, when the man noticed him.

"I know where you are from, little man," said the milkman in a quiet voice, thinking Timmy was a real tortoise. "You're a long way from home. I'd better give you a lift." He bent down, picked Timmy up, and put him in an empty box on the front seat. Timmy just sat there thinking it must be easier than crawling all the way home. He hoped the man really knew where he lived.

The milk float stopped and started all the way through the village. Timmy had fallen asleep again, tucked up nice and warm in his little box. He woke with a start as he felt the box move.

"I must be home," he thought, looking through a small hole in the box. "I am! I am!" he repeated to himself, full of excitement. "What a nice way to travel."

"Come on my little one; I'll take you round to the back," said the kind milkman.

He placed the box on the edge of the lawn and lifted Timmy out, saying, "Don't you wonder off again," before he picked up the empty box and his bottles and vanished into the darkness.

Timmy knew he was in the right place. He could see Jester sitting by the pond at the bottom of the garden. With a sly grin on his face, Timmy headed towards Jester, a little bit faster than he usually traveled.

"What an experience I've had tonight," remarked Timmy, as Jester acknowledged him with a smile. "There are so many kind people living here in Genom."

Idle Chatter

It was dull and overcast this morning. All the gnomes began to wake after their new experience last night when they all met in the park after dark in the play area, which had swings, a large slide, a climbing frame, a couple of roundabouts, and a small sandpit.

The first things Johnny thought of were the gates at the front of the house where they lived, which belonged to Mr and Mrs McCue. When Justin and Willy returned from last night's party, they noticed that, for some reason, the iron gates had been removed and laid against the hedge. Justin had said that Johnny hadn't kept a good enough watch – after all, he'd stayed in the garden all night to keep guard.

Johnny had heard the voice of Mr McCue and wasn't alarmed, but Justin's remarks made him worry all through the night, in case he hadn't done his job properly.

Now he sneaked off to the front of the house and sighed with relief when he saw two men rubbing the gates with wire brushes to take off the paint. He scanned the area and noticed tins of paint set to one side. Now he knew there was nothing to worry about. The men were shouting to each other over the noise of a radio positioned on the drive. One of the workmen started to whistle along to a tune being played.

He rushed back to tell Willy and Johnny. The look of relief on his face said it all.

Next door, in the Temperton's garden, Timmy the tortoise was telling his story to Mustafa and his friends about how he got a lift home in the milkman's float, saving him time and effort. Timmy couldn't express his gratitude enough for the way the kind milkman had treated him.

With all the gnomes swapping stories from the night before, nobody had noticed that poor old Lofty was back at his post, standing proudly, holding on to his wheelbarrow in the middle of the lawn.

"Look!" Ella said excitedly. "Lofty's back. He's got a new jacket on."

"All they've done is given me a new coat of paint to cover the crack in my arm," Lofty said. "It's nice to be out in the fresh air again. I don't suppose I've missed much!"

"Not really," Sam answered, "although we've got the new tree, and we had a brilliant party last night in the park."

"Oh thank you guys for letting me know! I would have loved to come," Lofty replied. "I bet you never even thought of me, locked away in that shed."

"I did!" Ella squealed. "*I* missed you. I wanted you to push me on the swings, but I ended up with Plank."

"Never mind. Possibly next time," Jester said, butting in.

"I can't stay around here all day. I must go and see if everybody got home all right," Raymond the rabbit said, as he hopped off into the distance.

"Did I tell you how *I* got home?" shouted Timmy to Raymond.

Ray stopped in his tracks at the corner of the house, turned, and shouted back, "You've told me at least twice. I'm off, see you all later."

Raymond was away on his travels again, exploring the village. There were parts he still had not seen.

Jimmy and Justin decided to have a wander themselves, leaving Willy, the eldest, and Johnny to have a rest.

They heard the rippling sound of the water in the stream lapping over the stones and headed down to investigate.

"This bank is rather steep," Justin said, picking his steps very carefully.

"Just take it easy. Nice and slow. That's it," Jimmy said, holding onto Justin's arm.

"We've made it. That wasn't too bad, was it?" Justin said, breathing slowly.

They headed on upstream. Everything looked different:

clean looking, vivid colours from the trees and flowers that were growing wild along the river bank.

"Hello, where are you two going?" The voice came from behind a large bush.

"Hello! You made us jump. We're just out for a walk, checking out the area," Justin said, recognising Raymond, who was with Button and Plank.

"Don't tell me! *You* come here everyday," smiled Jimmy.

"Not really, I was just on my travels and bumped into Button, who asked what was down here, so I said I'd show him, and Plank tagged along," Raymond told him.

"We might as well join you, if you don't mind, because this is all new to us, and, of course, you know your way round or you should do by now," Justin said.

* * * * *

Mrs McCue walked into Mr and Mrs Temperton's

garden and knocked on the back door.

Mrs Temperton opened the door with a welcoming smile. "Hello Joyce. Nice to see you, come on in," she said politely.

"Thank you very much, but I won't come in. I just wondered how you're getting on with this competition for the most beautiful village. My husband is driving me mad. He never stops talking about it," Mrs McCue remarked.

"Not too bad. My husband's got Jack to help him. He's very good in the garden and round the house too," Mrs Temperton said. "Are you sure you won't come in?"

"No I won't. It's my washing day, and I'm just waiting for the washing machine to finish. With this wind, it should be a good drying day too."

"Well, just sit here for a minute. I haven't seen you for such a long time," Mrs Temperton said, pointing to the wooden bench outside the door.

They both sat on the bench in the midday sun, talking

away for what seemed like ages, chatting about this and that, and talking about people that they've never met.

Lofty, standing in the middle of the garden, could hear everything that was being said. He pricked up his ears when he heard a story of an old lady who lived alone, just opposite Mrs McCue's, who would like to enter the competition but who was a little bit too old to be bending down cleaning the flower beds, pruning the trees, and pulling up all the weeds.

"Mrs Hardie, that's the little old lady, thinks the competition is a good way of getting all the villagers to tidy up their gardens. She contacted the local scout group to see if they could help, but unfortunately they all go off to camp tomorrow, somewhere up in North Yorkshire; so they can't help her," Mrs McCue said.

"The whole competition is a good idea. It's bringing the people of the village together, and it will certainly improve the look of the village. It's just that the men are taking it too seriously," Mrs Temperton remarked.

"Tell me about it! All I hear about on an evening when my husband comes back from the hotel after meeting his friends over a drink is the competition," sighed Mrs McCue. "Hopefully, it will soon be over, unless the village goes forward into the next round, which means more work for us all!"

"What do you mean?" Mrs Temperton asked.

"If the village wins in the area heats, we go forward to the county competition," Mrs McCue continued.

The two women forgot what time it was and sat in the sun, catching up on old times.

Meanwhile, Justin, Jimmy, Raymond, Button, and Plank continued on their venture along the bank of the stream. They couldn't believe the colours of all the different plants and shrubs that were growing wild along the path.

Plank asked, "Why, if these plants are growing wild, can't we pick some and re-plant them in our gardens?"

"I don't know about that," Button said, holding firmly

onto his jacket, in case he got caught on a tree branch and lost his last remaining button.

"Oh look at the time," squealed Mrs McCue. "I'm going to have to go, and I've got a list of jobs as long as my arm to get through today. We'll have to catch up on everything another time."

Thanking Mrs Temperton, she rushed away.

Lofty had a lot to think about. He couldn't help overhearing the two ladies' conversation. His main concern was the little old lady across the road, who needed help with tidying up her garden.

When it was all quiet, he sent a signal to Timmy the tortoise, who was sitting under Sam and Ella's mushroom, which protected him from the sun's rays. He looked so comfortable in the shade.

Timmy noticed Lofty's signal and made his way very slowly across the lawn to nestle down under Lofty's heavy wheelbarrow.

"I've heard that there's a little old lady who lives over the road, and she'd like her garden to look like the rest in the village. She can't do it herself and the local scout group have gone away. I think it would make an ideal project for all the Gnomes of Genom to club together and do the work for her after she's gone to bed," Lofty said in a very excited voice. "Can you go and mention it to Mustafa and then let me know?"

Timmy slowly made his way back across the lawn, panting as he went. He thought that he had already done a day's work.

"Come on Timmy, speed up a little bit," Lofty said, noticing the sad look on his face.

"Gnomebody knows how hard it is for me to travel over rough ground. Gnomematter how many times I tell them," Timmy said to himself.

Justin, Jimmy, and friends returned from their adventure along the bank and decided to have a rest whilst Raymond hopped off to see what else he could find of interest in the sleepy village.

Timmy the tortoise spent some time discussing Lofty's idea with Mustafa. Eventually, they agreed that it was a good idea and decided to get Raymond to mention it to all the other gnomes, but they couldn't find Raymond.

They pondered on the idea for a little bit longer, while sitting on the edge of a pile of grass cuttings. Timmy told Mustafa that he must be one of the oldest ornaments in the village and that he was pleased when Mustafa arrived and changed their world.

Time passed by and Raymond returned.

"Where have you been?"

"I've been all over the place just checking to see if everybody was all right after last night," Raymond said, feeling a little bit guilty.

"Well, we've got another job for you. Can you go and tell all the others to meet here later tonight and be ready to do some work?" Timmy asked, feeling proud and in control.

"What's it all about? They're going to ask questions. I want to be ready with the right answers," Raymond said.

"Well, it's like this…"

Mustafa relayed to Raymond Lofty's idea about how they could do a makeover on old Mrs Hardie's garden whilst she was asleep.

"That's a brilliant idea," remarked Raymond. "I've found something that will be of great use to us tonight in our task. This afternoon, I spotted something in that old lady's garden. Bright green it was. Just standing there as if it had nothing to do." Raymond was getting excited.

"What *are* you talking about?" Timmy asked.

"A train!" said Ray, "called Dwain. Dwain the train. He told me that he used to be in the garden of the Genom Green Hotel, just sitting on a bridge overlooking the stream. He lost count of how many years he had been there, just going rusty, when all of a sudden, he woke up covered in a nice new coat of green paint in Mrs Hardie's garden. I told him that the same thing had happened to us when the Star of Light changed our world. He seemed very grateful. Anyway, I was down by the stream this morning with Jimmy and his pals. They were surprised by all the bright colours on the bank, and Plank asked why we couldn't pick them and put them in our gardens. It's all falling into place. Why don't we get Dwain to pull his carriages down to the stream, pick all the wild flowers, put them onto the train, and plant them in Mrs Hardie's garden? It will certainly bring some colour and life back into it."

"Don't you think we could be going a bit too far?" Timmy asked.

"Not at all," Mustafa said. "It's going to make our job that little bit easier. Our purpose is to make Mrs Hardie happy. Yes, it *is* going to surprise her, but, in the long run, it's going to keep the Gnomes of Genom busy and make a close bond between us all."

In his "firm" voice, which was understood to be an

order, Mustafa told Dwain to get his engine steamed up and ready for tonight.

"I must report back to Lofty," Timmy shouted. "He'll be pleased that we've accepted his idea."

Lofty's Idea

Mustafa spent the rest of the day thinking of how he could take control of the situation and carry out Lofty's idea of doing a makeover of Mrs Hardie's garden while she was asleep.

Lofty overheard Mrs Temperton and Mrs McCue talking in the garden this morning about how Mrs Hardie would love to enter the garden competition, but she lives alone and is quite elderly. She had asked the local scout group for their help, but unfortunately they were away at camp for a week somewhere in Yorkshire and couldn't help; so Lofty thought that the Gnomes of Genom would love to help her out without her knowing.

Mustafa agreed, thinking that it would make a bond between them all, especially all working together, but it would have to be done properly.

Mustafa had a plan at the back of his mind that when

they all met again, he could split the workforce into two: one half to prepare Mrs Hardie's garden by digging up all the weeds, cutting the lawn, and preparing the flower beds, whilst the other half could go down to the stream and collect wild plants and flowers.

Mustafa noticed Raymond arriving back from his travels.

"Have you seen Dwain?" he asked.

"Yes," he replied. "He'll start to get steamed up with his engine just when the sun starts to go down. He's so exited! After all the years of just sitting around going rusty, he can get back to working again. I've asked Simon and Plank to go round earlier with some oil that I found to put on Dwain's wheels, because they look as though they haven't turned in ages."

"Good thinking," approved Mustafa. "How many do you think will turn up tonight?"

"Far more than you think. Everyone thinks it's a brilliant

idea."

Mustafa pondered who could do what and decided to go into Mrs Hardie's garden to have a look for himself to see what exactly was going to be involved. Before he set off, he took a close look behind him. He could see the stream from where he sat and noticed all the vivid colours that he hadn't noticed before.

"Where has Raymond gone now?" he asked Jester in a quizzing voice. Jester was looking at his reflection in the pond.

"I saw him talking to Sam and Ella a few minutes ago, and then they all went off in a hurry," Jester replied. "It's not fair on Lofty and me. *We've* been placed so that we can be seen at all times. *We* just can't wander off when we feel like it. Sometimes I just feel like throwing down my rod and trotting off to talk to Lofty to see how he feels."

"I'm just going to have a look at Mrs Hardie's garden, so if Raymond comes back, keep him here if you can," Mustafa asked him.

Raymond, Sam, and Ella had arrived at the gates of Green End Farm where they used to live.

"I'm not too sure about this," Ella said doubtfully to the other two.

"Come on. All we're going to do is have a look and see what's changed. It'll only take a few minutes," Sam said, reassuring his sister.

They went into the farm very gingerly, trying not to make a sound and hoping that nobody would hear them.

"Oh look Ella!" whispered Sam. "We used to sit just over there in front of the sheep pen. Let's go and have a look. Let's see if we can recognise any of them."

They both ran off. No sound was coming from the pens, so they peeked through a crack in the wall but found nothing.

"All the sheep must be out in the fields. They won't be back inside for ages. What a shame!" Ella said.

"Just let me go round the back and have a look. I should

be able to see the field from there," whispered Sam.

"All right, but don't be long. Don't forget we shouldn't be here," Ella said quietly.

Raymond hopped up behind Ella while she was making her jump.

"Oh, you startled me! Have you found the cows?" Ella asked.

"I've found the shed, but they all must be out grazing," gasped an out-of-breath Raymond.

"I saw two men cleaning the shed with a hosepipe, so I didn't want to stay too long," Raymond continued. "Where's Sam?"

"He's just gone round the back to see if he can see the fields, because the sheep aren't here either," Ella told him.

Sam returned with a big smile on his face.

"Yes, they're all in the fields, grazing away like anything," he said.

"We ought to be getting back. Gnomebody knows where we are," remarked Raymond. "And we have a long night ahead of us."

Mustafa went into Mrs Hardie's garden through a large hole in the hedge. He was amazed at the size and the state of it and wondered whether they had bitten off more than they could chew. It was going to take a lot of work to make this place into a lovely garden, but it would be a challenge.

While he was looking around, more and more ideas came into his head. He slowly convinced himself that it could be done with the help of his friends. The ideas were flowing thick and fast now. "We could even build a rockery perhaps!" he said to himself.

There were lots of broken flower pots lying around, ranging from very large to small, colourful ones. Mustafa thought to himself that he should use these broken pots as a feature in a corner of the garden, with plants flowing over them. He wandered around, taking a mental note of everything.

Strolling back across the road, more and more images of the new garden appeared in his mind. He was determined to see a great result.

Seeing Raymond with Sam and Ella, Mustafa asked them, "Where have you three been?"

"We've just been to the other end of the village and had a look in the farm – Green End Farm. We all used to live there, looking after the cows and sheep," answered Ella in a low, whispering voice.

"I hope you were careful and nobody saw you," Mustafa said.

"We were," Raymond said. "All the cows and sheep were in the fields, so we didn't get to see them."

"OK, but next time, please let me know where you're going," Mustafa said in a firm voice. "I'm trying to organise things for tonight, and I don't want people just wandering around."

"I did find a lot of grass turf behind the sheep pen, which I think has just been left there, along with lots of odd bits of wood, which might come in handy tonight," Sam offered.

"We can always get Dwain to go and pick it up after he's been to collect the flowers," Raymond said.

"I'll bear it in mind. I have a lot to think about at the moment." Mustafa turned and walked towards the McCue's house, hoping to find Willy, so that he could discuss his ideas. Willy was one of the eldest gnomes and has done a fair bit of travelling. Mustafa was going to ask him if he would like to be in charge of collecting the flowers and showing Dwain the way round.

You could feel the excitement in the air as evening approached. The Gnomes of Genom couldn't wait to get to work.

They all arrived in the Temperton's garden, carrying as much equipment as they could and eager for their instructions.

Mustafa got to his feet. Everybody stopped chattering and looked at him, their eagerness showing on their faces.

Mustafa started by thanking them all for turning up.

"I've had a chance to look at Mrs Hardie's garden. There's going to be a lot of hard work required, but I'm sure you'll all do your best," he continued. "I've put Willy in charge of collecting the flowers and things from the bank of the stream, so if six of you could go with him," Mustafa said. Then, he stopped suddenly. "Oh. I'm sorry, Dwain! I haven't introduced you to the clan. Everyone, this is Dwain, the train we found in Mrs Hardie's garden. He used to work at the hotel at the other end of the village, but, for some reason, woke up across the road from here when the Star of Life was born. He'll help Willy transport the plants and flowers and take a trip to the farm to collect some spare grass turf that we might use. The rest of you can come with me to prepare the ground so it will be ready for Dwain's arrival."

"I can't stress enough, the importance of this project,

both to Mrs Hardie and us. We must always remember the pleasure Mrs Hardie will get out of her garden and the pleasure we will get out of doing it. Let's hope that this project will be a great success." Mustafa stood there proudly.

"Come on lads, let's get to work," shouted Willy.

Jimmy, Justin, Sam, Ella, Plank, and Button joined Willy in one of Dwain's carriages and waved goodbye to the rest. They looked as though they were going on holiday the way they were leaning out of the windows with wide smiles on their faces.

The rest picked up their tools, slung them over their shoulders, and formed a line behind Mustafa. They were ready for the command to start walking, just like the seven dwarfs in the fairy tale but without the whistling.

Raymond of course had sped off in front of all the others. He had always wanted to be the first to arrive, and he was quicker than the rest.

After getting into Mrs Hardie's garden through the hole in the hedge, the working party started to clear the area. It was really overgrown at the bottom of the garden with huge weeds.

Simon and Lofty began pulling up weeds, while Timmy the tortoise slowly moved the lightweight stones and piled them in a corner.

"Bon soir, Monsieur!" said a voice from under the stones.

Timmy tripped over with fright. "Hey! Who are you?"

"I'm Pierre. I come from a country called France," he said with a tremor in his voice.

Lofty idled across towards Timmy. "What's going on?" he asked.

"I was moving the stones as I was told when I discovered Pierre. He's from France," Timmy replied.

Pierre emerged further out from under the stones. His clothes were different from the rest of the gnomes in the village. He had a black- and white-striped shirt, with a red scarf, black trousers, and a black hat rather like Willie's pulled across his forehead to just above his eyebrows.

"How did you get here then?" Lofty asked.

"I've been here for years, tucked away in this part of the garden. I became hidden behind all this grass, and the old lady must have forgotten about me. I believe one of the neighbours went to France on holiday and brought me back as a present for the lady who lives here," Pierre replied.

"You've got lots of smelly things hanging round your neck! What are those?" Timmy asked.

"These are called onions," replied Pierre pointing to his garland round his neck. "We eat them in France. Many people grow them in their gardens."

Lofty said sternly, "Here in this village, all we grow are nice-looking colourful plants. We leave things like onions to the farmers, along with the sheep and cows. While you are here, you might as well help us out, seeing you live here. We're upgrading the garden as a surprise for Mrs Hardie."

"I've also got a friend hidden in that old plant pot over there," Pierre said, pointing to a dull orange pot just behind them. "He's from Spain, and his name is Juan."

"How many more of you are there?" Timmy enquired.

As Pierre answered, "That's it. Just Juan and me," Juan appeared from under the pot, simply dressed in the same-coloured hat and jacket as Lofty.

"Buenos dias, Senor," Juan said, holding his hand out in friendship towards Lofty.

"Hello," Lofty replied, with a frown on his face, as he didn't understand a word of what Juan had said. "Come on. We've wasted enough time. Let's get on with the job. We'll talk later when we have a rest. So if you two want to help Timmy, I'll go back over there."

Meanwhile, down near the stream, Dwain had come to

a halt.

"Willy is there another way we can get down?" shouted Dwain, as he realised that the bank was too steep. "My brakes aren't that good. We could end up in the stream if we aren't careful."

"Ay laddie, there is, but it means a long detour," Willy remarked with frustration in his voice.

"Come on, show me the way. We haven't got all night. We've got two or three runs to do," said Dwain the train. He reversed and headed back through the Temperton's garden towards the main road while pulling his carriages. When they reached the road, they turned left, headed out of the village, and passed a small corner shop, which seemed to have everything in the window.

Clickerty clack, clickerty clack go the wheels as they rode the cracks in the pavement.

"Turn left just here," Willy said, pointing to a narrow walkway between the houses.

Dwain turned and headed towards the stream, puffing slowly along. They arrived near the stream, only to find they were further upstream than they thought.

"When we stop, I'm going to need a lot more wood to put into my tender. I didn't think we'd be going this far," remarked Dwain, still puffing.

"That's no problem," Plank said. "We're enjoying the ride. We'll collect as much wood as you want."

Dwain slowly steamed along the side of the stream, until they arrived just below the bottom of Mr and Mrs Temperton's garden.

"Before we start loading up, do you think you should turn around Dwain, because we'll have to go back the same way as we came?" Justin suggested, who seemed very quiet.

"That's good thinking. I thought you were asleep," Willy said, stretching himself.

Dwain began to turn himself around while the rest,

except for Jimmy and Button, went to work picking plants and flowers, choosing all the brightly coloured ones. Jimmy and Button searched the hedgerows for the extra wood that Dwain would need to complete his journey. When the train was loaded up with as much as he could carry, he slowly moved off in the same direction as he came, towards Mrs Hardie's garden.

Meanwhile, the activity there had been intense. Everybody had been very busy. The whole garden area had been cleared of unwanted items, except for one corner where Mustafa and Timmy, with the help of Lofty and his wheelbarrow, had built a great big rockery with all the large rocks and stones they'd found just lying around.

"That wheelbarrow of yours does come in useful Lofty," Mustafa remarked, rubbing his hands together to get some of the dirt off.

"You're right," Lofty said. "There is no way you could have moved all those rocks and soil without me. I've enjoyed it; it's been worthwhile. Let's hope that Willy has picked some nice bright colours."

Mustafa and his friends also uncovered a rock pool that made another feature for the garden where birds could come and have a bath in their natural surroundings. Mustafa stood back and scratched his head, while looking at the progress made so far. His face began to light up, when all of a sudden, he jumped in the air shouting, "I've got it! I've got it! I really think I've got it!"

Dwain approached, giving a short whistle to alert them of his arrival. Mustafa ran towards them grabbing hold of Willy. "Come on," he said to Willy, "I've got this excellent idea! I'd like to discuss it with you, Pierre, and Juan to finalise the details."

The four of them went to a remote corner of the garden to discuss Mustafa's new idea, while the rest unpacked the train so that Dwain could go back to the other end of the village.

Mrs Hardie's Delight

The Gnomes of Genom were enjoying working in Mrs Hardie's garden and giving it a makeover, unbeknownst to the little old lady who was fast asleep in her pretty cottage.

Dwain, the old rusty train who Mustafa had found in the garden, had set off to Green End Farm with the twins, Sam and Ella, to collect whatever he could find lying around that might come in handy to decorate the new garden. He had already made one journey down to the stream, returning with colourful wild plants that had been already unloaded by the gnomes.

Scottish Willy, French Pierre, and Spanish Juan gathered in a corner of the garden with Mustafa to listen to his new plan.

"It just came to me when I was looking around the area.

I don't know why I didn't think of it before, but you two have made all the difference," an excited Mustafa turned to Pierre and Juan.

"What are you going on about?" Willy asked.

"It's simple. Why don't we divide the garden into four different sections. We could have a Scottish one, a French area, and a Spanish one, leaving the last section as a typical English garden."

"Can you describe what Scotland is like Willy?" Mustafa asked.

"Well, it's a lovely country with rolling hills and mountains, lots of lakes, and very green," Willy told him.

Mustafa asked Pierre and Juan the same question, and they told him in detail what their countries were like: similar to Scotland as it turned out but much flatter and with different landmarks.

"I think we could make it work; we could give each area a different look around the rock pool in the middle. You could imagine the pool as a lake for Scotland and France and as the sea for Spain or just a fish pond for the typical English garden. You see the rockery we've made over there," continued Mustafa, pointing to a great pile of soil and stones, "well, Raymond's found an old dog kennel. I thought that if we dig a hole in the rockery, put the kennel in the hole, and cover it with earth except for the opening, Dwain could sit in it. He'd look as though he's coming out of a railway tunnel, and, if we can find some rails, he'd be able to ride round the garden, passing through the different countries."

"It beats me," Willy said admiringly, "where you get all these ideas from."

"I'm not really sure," Mustafa said, "but I think it has something to do with the garden centre where I came from. I think they called it Grahams Garden Centre. I remember sitting in a beautifully landscaped garden, where they changed the theme every month. There were windmills, fountains, small plastic houses, and plastic animals. You name it, and it was there. The workmen were very good at their jobs."

"It seems like a good idea to me," Juan said in his Spanish accent.

"What are we waiting for? Let's get on with it," Pierre said excitedly.

With their agreement, Mustafa went round to all the other gnomes and explained the new plan with the help of Juan and Pierre.

There seemed to be a new enthusiasm among them as they began to work even harder and faster than before.

When Dwain and the twins arrived at the farm, everything was in darkness except for a glimmer of light near the chicken coops.

"Don't worry about that light," Ella said. "That's where they hatch the new chicks. We won't go anywhere near there."

"Well, where *do* we start? Don't forget I need to turn

around," Dwain reminded them, still puffing and panting.

"We could go round in a large circle starting behind the sheep pen. The sheep are out in the fields, so we won't disturb them. I know there are some pieces of turf just behind there. We ought to collect as much as we can. Anything that we could use. We can always bring it back," Sam said.

Dwain got steam up and slowly moved around the farm, starting behind the sheep pen, then to an old barn that was full of machinery like tractors and ploughs, and through the main yard ending up at the cow shed. Sam and Ella had been jumping on and off the train all night collecting anything they could carry.

"I hear that you two used to live here once upon a time," Dwain said. "I think Raymond was here as well. I used to be at the Genom Green Hotel, just down the road. We passed it on the way. We might as well go and have a look and see if any of my old things are still left," he added with a pleading look on his face.

"Why not? We might as well, seeing we're at this end of the village," Ella said, stifling a yawn.

Back in Mrs Hardie's garden, the clan were all busy rushing around. Each one had their own little job to do. They didn't have time to stand and chat or even dare interfere in anybody else's job.

Suddenly, Plank shouted, "SHUSH everybody! I can hear a dog barking. It's coming from the cottage."

A light appeared in the upstairs bedroom, which shined brighter as the curtains were pulled to one side. The gnomes saw a figure peering out of the window.

"Hide, hide everybody," Mustafa shouted, running for cover behind the dustbin.

Mrs Hardie peered out from behind the curtain. "It's all dark. I can't see anything," she said, turning and looking at her faithful dog who woke her up with his barking.

The dog barked again followed by a short whimper. "All right, we'll go and have a look," said the old lady. "Come on Rufus, if you're coming," she called as she walked out of the bedroom door.

All the gnomes had now hidden themselves; they were shaking and trembling with fear, hoping that they wouldn't be spotted.

They could hear the bolts on the back door being shot back and the key turning in the lock.

Rufus came scampering out. He was black apart from white markings on his stomach. He was a small dog, with a curly tail – just like a pig's tail that twists on itself. He could sense new smells in the air. With his tail wagging, he kept his nose firmly to the ground, moving quickly around the garden, while Mrs Hardie stood at the back door.

"Come on Rufus; let's go back to bed," Mrs Hardie shouted.

She turned and made her way into the kitchen, leaving the door slightly open so that Rufus could come back in.

Heading towards the door, Rufus stopped near the

dustbin. He had picked up the scent of Mustafa.

"Shush," Mustafa said, as he met Rufus face to face, "don't bark anymore. We're only here to help."

Rufus replied in a whimpering voice, "I know, but I didn't expect to see you tonight. Dwain told me all about it. How are you going to improve the garden for nice Mrs Hardie?"

Jester appeared from under a table. "You're a talking dog, and I can understand you," he said laughing as he always did. "You could help us by keeping quiet and keeping the old lady in the cottage until we are finished."

"I'll do my best, but promise me that if you find any old bones, you'll just leave them in a pile for me over by the hedge," replied Rufus, licking his lips.

Rufus stood there for a moment, sniffing the air before returning inside the cottage to play his part in helping the gnomes.

Everything was quiet once more. The Gnomes of

Genom returned to work.

The twins and Dwain had now arrived at the hotel. They made their way to the back of the building.

"What a big place this is," remarked Sam, looking at the well-kept garden that seemed to spread as far as he could see. "I'm glad we don't have to do any work on this one."

"That was my shed over there," Dwain said, pointing to a hut that had obviously aged over the years.

By this time, Ella was beginning to get very tired. "Come on! Let's do what we have to. The rest will be waiting for us."

Dwain headed for his old shed, hoping to find some of his old belongings.

Disappointment showed on his face when he found the shed full of golf equipment. Taking a quick look outside, he saw that part of the lawn had been turned into a 9-hole putting green for the hotel guests.

"Oh well, it was worth a try," he said. "It must be a few years since I sat in this garden anyway."

Moving off slowly, they headed back to Mrs Hardie's garden to see what progress had been made.

Rufus gave out a little bark as he heard Dwain give a short hoot on his whistle.

Arriving at the cottage, they were amazed at what greeted them.

The whole garden had been transformed. They could hardly believe their eyes. It was now laid out in four sections with different-coloured plants in each section.

"I must say, it looks very tidy and colourful," Sam remarked.

"What a difference! I can't believe it!" Dwain said, looking at Mustafa who was covered in mud.

"What have you been able to collect?" Willy asked, making his way to the back of the train.

Everyone gathered round to help unload.

"Hey Willy! Come here!" Raymond shouted.

"D'you remember our little secret? You know what we found in the park? That mirror?"

"Yes, of course," Willy replied.

"Well, we could use it as a lake. We could put it between some small shrubs, with some reeds laid over the side. From a distance, it would look just like a stretch of water, especially when the sun shines on it. We could even make a small boat out of wood," Raymond continued.

"Do you remember where we left it?" Willy asked.

"I think so," Raymond replied. "I'll go and get it."

Within seconds, he had hopped off into the night.

The gnomes continued unloading the train and putting to use anything that they could, while Plank and Button started to lay the grass turf in the Scottish section to make it look as though the landscape had hills that rolled up and down far into the distance.

Jester and Juan were busy breaking stones and then

rubbing them together to make a powder that would look like sand to place round the pond and to represent the beaches of Spain.

Pierre was huddled in one corner, building what looked like a large tower.

The rest were busy tidying up and repositioning the flowers and plants, while Willy tried to unravel the hosepipe so that when it was all finished, they could give everything a good soaking.

"I presume that's for me," Dwain said, noticing the new tunnel.

"Of course," Mustafa told him. "We couldn't let you just sit around going rusty again, could we?"

Raymond returned with the mirror and explained to Mustafa all about how they found it and how they could use it.

"Brilliant! That will just finish it off," Mustafa said.

Daylight was slowly approaching. The gnomes had

finished, and Willy was just hosing everything down. Dwain took up his position in the tunnel, looking out over his new domain.

* * * * * *

Morning arrived and, as usual, Mrs Hardie came into the kitchen to put the kettle on while she went back to her bedroom to get washed and dressed. She didn't know what had been going on during the night, although Rufus, her little dog, couldn't wait to get out in the garden to see what improvements the gnomes had made.

Rufus sat by the back door whining to go out. This was unusual. He always waited until Mrs Hardie had finished her breakfast.

He decided to be patient and not to hurry Mrs Hardie. He just layed on the back door mat with his face resting on his front paws with a slight glimpse of eagerness on his face.

Minutes later his patience was been rewarded; Mrs

Hardie had her breakfast and had washed up. "Come on Rufus," she said, "it's time you went out."

Rufus didn't waste any time. He was outside like a rocket. He went straight to the dustbin and sniffed around the base to see if Mustafa was still there. He found nothing! Bounding down to the bottom of the garden, he noticed Dwain in the tunnel.

"What a fantastic job you've done," Rufus said, sniffing the new fragrances that were drifting through the air from the flowers.

"I only played a small part in the operation. It's all down to the Gnomes of Genom and Mustafa's idea," retorted Dwain, smiling at Rufus. "I hope you like it. I think *I* can live with it."

Mrs Hardie stepped out, into the morning sunshine.

"Oh my word! What *has* happened," she cried with tears appearing in her eyes. "I can't believe it! It's lovely!"

The old lady slowly walked round her new garden,

muttering to herself as she went. Rufus was now walking by her side, still taking in the new smells.

"Rufus, d'you know who's done this?" she asked looking down at him.

Rufus jumped up and put his front paws on her thigh, holding his head to one side as though to say, "everything's all right."

Mrs Hardie felt as though she had to tell someone about the mystic happening. She walked inside, picked up the telephone, and dialed the number of the Reverend Alf Johnson, the vicar who lived in the next village.

There was no reply, so she put her shoes on and dashed across the road to Mrs McCue's house. She had to tell someone.

She left so quickly that she forgot about Rufus. The little black dog had wandered around the garden so many times and sniffed so many flowers and plants that he didn't realise that Mrs Hardie had gone.

Not at all worried, he decided to go and congratulate Mustafa and his friends. He left the garden through the hole in the hedge – the same one that the gnomes used during the night. It had been made much larger with all the comings and goings. Rufus ran straight across the road with his ears plastered flat to his head, his name tag rattling against his collar, and his curly tail flattened by his speed.

"Mustafa! Mustafa!" he shrieked. "She loves it! She really loves it!"

"Thank goodness," replied Mustafa. "We loved doing it. I'm glad it's been worthwhile."

Gnomebody Knows

Mrs Hardie, the little old lady who lived in the cottage just across the road from Mrs McCue, couldn't believe what had been done to her garden. When she went to bed, her garden was overgrown. It was a mess. It had been neglected for such a long time, mainly because she couldn't look after it herself. However, she had also been desperate to enter the village garden competition.

She didn't want to disappoint the other villagers who had really worked hard on *their* gardens by not doing anything. She'd been a very isolated member of the village community ever since she arrived. She wasn't the kind of lady who'd get involved in village life by inviting people round for coffee and talking about people she didn't know. Now this was her chance to get to know more villagers.

But who had been in her garden?

And *why* had they done it?

Who *are* these people?

Mrs Hardie was so pleased with the makeover of her garden that she had to tell someone. She was so excited that she put on her shoes and rushed out of the front door, forgetting to lock it, and headed across the road to Mrs McCue's house.

Rufus was left in the garden on his own, wandering around looking at all the changes that Mustafa and his friends had made. He often stopped and sniffed the air, which was full of all the new smells from the plants and flowers.

Turning to Dwain, Rufus remarked, "What a fantastic job you've done. You warned me that something was going to happen, but I didn't expect this. It's great."

"It's surprising what you can do when you put your mind to it, especially with the right organisation, and, I must say, Mustafa is a good organiser. Oh, you won't know, but Pierre and Juan, those old statues that were hidden underneath a lot of the rubbish, helped as well – hence the theme of France and Spain along with Scotland."

By this time, Rufus was so excited he had gone scampering off through the hole in the hedge to congratulate Mustafa. His ears were flattened to the side of his head, and his curly tail was straightened by his speed.

Dwain was standing proudly in his new tunnel, looking out over the newly formed landscape. He was also astonished at what the gnomes had achieved. The look of satisfaction on his face said it all.

Mrs Hardie rapped very loudly in her excitement on Mrs McCue's front door. She appeared in the doorway within seconds.

"Hello Mrs Hardie, what can I do for you?" she asked. "Do you need any help?"

"Not at all! You wouldn't believe it, but I've had enough help in the last twelve hours, and I don't know where it came from," Mrs Hardie replied. "May I come in so I can explain? I have to tell someone about it."

"Very well. You'd better come in, but I don't understand," Mrs McCue said.

"I was hoping that *you* knew something about last night," Mrs Hardie said, wiping her feet on the doormat.

"Come on in. I'll put the kettle on, and then you can tell me all about it," replied Mrs McCue, slowly shutting the door.

Mrs McCue made a pot of tea while old Mrs Hardie sat at the kitchen table thinking of how she could explain what had happened without sounding silly. She began to relate her story, and Mrs McCue listened intently.

Meanwhile, Rufus had found Mustafa talking to Jester and Raymond in the morning sunlight round the pond.

"What are *you* doing here?" asked Raymond.

"I had to come and tell you that you've done a brilliant job on the garden. Mrs Hardie can't believe it, and, to be honest, neither can I. She thinks it's lovely," said Rufus, still panting from his long run.

As they discussed their last night's handiwork, Jester noticed dark clouds building up overhead and reflecting in the pond.

"Oh dear, we're going to get a downpour. Those clouds are full of rain," he said, as spots of rain started rippling across his pond. "We ought to run for cover. I don't want to get soaked. I've had plenty of that, especially when I lost my float. Hee! Hee! D'you remember that Ray?"

Within seconds, the rain came down more heavily, and they rushed to join Sam and Ella under their mushroom. A big rumble of thunder could be heard in the distance.

"Oh, I don't like thunder and lighting," Ella said, moving closer to her brother.

"It's just what we wanted," came a little voice from under a pile of grass.

"Hello, Timmy! You've made it home then," Raymond

remarked.

"I've only just got back. It's taken me a long time. Anyway, I can sleep now, and nobody will disturb me," Timmy replied, slowly drawing his head into his shell.

"The rain will do old Mrs Hardie's garden a lot of good. It should help all the plants and flowers settle down," Mustafa remarked in his commanding voice.

A large flash flew across the darkened sky, followed by a crack of thunder.

Sam put his arm around his sister, saying, "I think it's getting closer, but you'll be all right."

The thunderstorm carried on for half an hour. Rain pelted down and bounced off the top of the mushroom where they were all sheltering. It made an echoing sound, which they found a little bit eerie.

Jester looked across the Temperton's garden and noticed poor old Lofty still holding onto his wheelbarrow; his hat was flattened against his head with the weight of the rain.

"Come on, Lofty!" Jester shouted. "Don't be silly! Come over here. It's a little bit drier."

Lofty thought to himself, "Why not? Gnomebody is going to see me!"

With that, he dropped his wheelbarrow and scampered towards the mushroom. After bending down and getting on his hands and knees, he said, "You'll have to move up a bit and give me some room."

They all huddled together, trying to give Lofty some space but only managed enough for his long body. His feet were still hanging out and getting wet.

"It's better than nothing," laughed Jester.

The sky got darker and darker, except for when the lighting flashed. The gnomes hadn't encountered anything like this before.

Timmy poked his head out of his shell. "Can you all remember what changed our lives?" he said with a questioning tone in his voice, trying to stifle a yawn. "It was a flash of light, just like that last one, which hit a remote star and changed our way of life completely. I hope those flashes aren't going to change things back again. I'm quite happy the way we are."

"Come on Timmy! The first flash was a manmade spark from Mr Temperton's barbecue, not a flash of lighting made by the clouds." Mustafa tried to console his friends, crossed his fingers behind his back, and said a prayer to himself and hoped that Timmy's theory wasn't right.

Mrs McCue listened to Mrs Hardie's story as the rain lashed down outside. The old lady still couldn't believe it even after she had told the whole story to Mrs McCue. She kept repeating herself. "I just can't believe it! It's lovely! It's really lovely!"

Mrs McCue was puzzled by what she had heard.

"I'll have to see it for myself," she said. "It sounds unbelievable! Are you sure it isn't a dream?"

"No! No! It's true, honestly!" answered Mrs Hardie,

getting more and more excited.

"Oh dear me," said Mrs McCue. "It can't be. No, it can't be!"

"What do you mean?" Mrs Hardie asked, sipping her cup of tea.

"I've just remembered. I went round to see Mrs Temperton the other day to see how *she* was coping with the garden competition, because my husband has been driving me mad. I happened to mention that you wanted to enter the competition, but you couldn't do the heavy work yourself. I even mentioned that you'd asked the local scouts for help. I wonder if *she* knows anything." Mrs McCue picked up a biscuit and rested it on her bottom lip with a thoughtful look on her face.

Mrs Hardie jumped up. "Come on, let's go and ask her."

"It's still raining. We'll wait until it's stopped," Mrs McCue said. "Would you like another cup of tea?"

Willy, the Scottish gnome, and his friends pushed through the hedge of the Temperton's garden, soaking wet from head to foot.

"It's all right for some," he remarked. "I wish *we* had a few mushrooms to shelter under, but I think it's nearly stopped. We were wondering if we could go and have another look at our handiwork from last night."

"I'll come with you," Rufus said. "Mrs Hardie has gone out and left the house unlocked. I really ought to be getting back, just in case somebody calls."

"Why don't we all go. We did leave in a hurry last night, and I didn't get time to wander around myself," Lofty said, trying to straighten his legs.

"Come on! Let's go! It's nearly stopped raining," urged Raymond, getting ready to hop off. He always liked to be the first to get anywhere.

The whole clan started moving; some were rushing, and some were taking their time just strolling along.

Tony Curtis

Mrs McCue and Mrs Hardie, who were both sharing a black umbrella, arrived at the back door of Mrs Temperton's house.

Mrs Hardie said to Mrs McCue in an embarrassed voice, "You'll have to introduce me. I've never spoken to this lady. I've only seen her walking through the village."

"Don't worry. They're a lovely couple. If they can help us, they will," Mrs McCue reassured her.

The two ladies entered Mrs Temperton's house after the introductions, and Mrs Temperton offered them a cup of tea.

"I'm not being rude, but I've had three cups already this morning," remarked Mrs Hardie, "but if you're having one, I might as well have another."

Mrs McCue outlined the whole story of how Mrs Hardie's garden had a makeover during the night and asked if Mrs Temperton knew anything about it.

"It sounds incredible, but I don't know anything about

it. All I remember is you telling me about Mrs Hardie's predicament. I'd love to come and have a look," said Mrs Temperton, frowning in disbelief. The ladies chatted away for another ten minutes. Mrs Temperton wanted to get to know her neighbour.

Meanwhile, back at Mrs Hardie's house, the gnomes had gathered in the garden.

"My, my, doesn't it look great," Lofty remarked.

"Ay laddie, it does. I must say, we've done a good job," Willy replied. "When are the judges coming round?"

"I think they visit all the gardens that have entered the competition tonight about teatime and then give the results tomorrow," Mustafa said.

"There's going to be a lot of busy gardeners this afternoon then," laughed Jester. "They'll all want to add those final touches. I hope the grass dries out, otherwise they won't be able to cut it after all that rain," he chuckled.

"At least the rain has helped *this* garden. There's nothing else we can do to it anyway," said Raymond, hopping down the garden to speak to Dwain.

Rufus was just sitting by the back door, looking out over the garden with a large grin on his face, when he had an idea.

Shouting to Mustafa, he said, "Look, Mrs Hardie's left the house open. Why don't we really finish the job off properly by cleaning the cottage from top to bottom. She'll never know it was us, and she's such a lovely lady. She's taken care of me. I would like to repay her somehow, and I didn't get involved in helping with the garden.

"Why not? That's a good idea. If a job's worth doing, it's worth doing properly," Ella agreed.

All the gnomes except Willy and Rufus went into the house and got to work. They had never met old Mrs Hardie, but they were prepared to help her out in any way possible. Cleaning the cottage shouldn't take long, because there were so many of them. The only problem was that there weren't enough dusters to go round; so, some of them started moving the furniture around to make more living space.

Willy and Rufus were busy walking around the garden, noticing things that they hadn't seen before like the mirror that was positioned to look like a lake, the sand on the beach, and the tower that was made out of some old wood.

Rufus had only noticed the new smells before coming from all the new flowers, which were neatly laid out in their own sections.

Dwain remarked from inside his tunnel, "What a difference a night's work can make. You all must be very tired."

"Not at all," replied Willy. "You only seem to get tired if you don't enjoy your work. We all really enjoyed doing it last night – so much that the rest are in the cottage right now tidying that up as well."

"Oh no! Just stay where you are," shouted Mustafa from

the back door. "Never mind. It's too late! Try and hide if you can."

Mrs Hardie, Mrs Temperton, and Mrs McCue were coming into the garden through the side gate.

Seeing the garden for the first time, Mrs McCue remarked, "Oh my word! How wonderful! It's beautiful!"

Mrs Temperton couldn't believe her eyes. She turned her head in every direction, finally focusing on the garden pond.

"I've never seen anything like it! It certainly puts my husband's efforts to shame, and words just can't describe it. You say you have no idea who's done it?"

"None at all," replied Mrs Hardie, "but whoever did it, I'm certainly grateful."

"All I can say is that I hope you win the competition. Our husbands have been working very hard for the last month, building up to the competition. It would be an eye opener if a woman won," Mrs Temperton commented.

Willy was hiding behind a very thin, tall flower, and insects were hovering around the petals. One landed on his nose and started tickling him. He did not dare to move in case he was spotted. He just had to twitch his nose and hope that it would fly away. He couldn't bear it. The insect was crawling all over his face, which made the tickling worse. It nestled on one of his nostrils, which made him want to sneeze; he held his breath for as long as he could. Suddenly, he couldn't hold it back any longer. Willy sneezed with an almighty ATISHOO!!!

"Bless you!" Rufus shouted, sitting beside Mrs Hardie's feet.

"Rufus, did you say something?" Mrs Hardie asked.

Not knowing that Mrs Hardie and her friends could understand him, he replied. "I just said bless you to Willy. He just sneezed."

"Rufus, how long have you been able to talk?" Mrs Hardie asked.

Rufus not thinking, replied, "Well, ever since Mustafa and his friends arrived."

Mrs Hardie sat down on the grass next to her faithful dog, and said, "What are you going on about? Do you know something about last night, and who is this Mustafa?"

Willy knew that Rufus had got himself into a tight corner and decided to help him out.

"Hello, Mrs Hardie. I'm Willy, one of Mustafa's friends," he said, slowly emerging from behind his flower.

"Oh my goodness! A talking gnome as well!" Mrs McCue took a step backwards.

The gnomes in the cottage heard everything that was going on outside in the garden.

Jester turned to Mustafa, "What are we going to do? The people can understand everything we say. It's never happened before. Why's it changed?"

"I don't know. All I can think of is what Timmy said earlier, about the spark that started it all off and the lightening during the storm. Maybe a bolt of lightening has struck our Star of Life, making further changes to our little world. All we can do is admit that it was us who made the changes to the garden," Mustafa said. Turning to his friends, he continued, "Come on everybody. Let's go and see what happens."

They all trooped out into the garden, one by one, in a straight line.

Rufus ran towards them and told Mrs Hardie, "This is Mustafa and his friends. They've just finished cleaning your cottage."

The three ladies were lost for words; all they could do was look at each other in disbelief, with their mouths gaping open.

"Don't be afraid. We're only here to help. We didn't know you could understand us," Mustafa said, taking control of the situation.

Mrs Temperton looked down at the circle of gnomes

and said, "I know you. You're the gnome my husband and I bought from the garden centre a few weeks ago. We named you Mustafa, if I remember."

"Yes, you did," Mustafa replied in a stern voice. "It was on that sign you bought at the same time that said, 'Every Home Must Have A Gnome'. If you care to sit down, I'll try and explain."

"The grass is wet; we'll have to go inside," Mrs McCue said.

Mrs Hardie smiled and said, "It's my turn to put the kettle on."

They all turned towards the cottage when Jester began to laugh. It was that kind of chuckly laugh that makes everyone else laugh. They noticed Lofty was still in the cottage. He appeared at the kitchen window with a cloth in his hand; he was reaching high up into the corners with his long arms, still working and cleaning the window.

The gnomes' laughter spread to the three ladies. They

laughed so much that it made their tummies hurt. Jester had laughed so much it had made his eyes water, as tears rolled down his rosy cheeks. Timmy was on his back with his legs in the air, rolling from side to side, whilst Raymond was hopping around. He just couldn't keep still, chuckling away to himself. Willy took his hat off to wipe his eyes, displaying a small bald patch at the back of his head. Mustafa pointed at Willy's bald patch, breaking out into more laughter. It was the first time they had seen him without that stupid sponge on his head, and they didn't know he was bald.

Rufus' tail had nearly dropped off with all the wagging he had done. His tongue was hanging out of his mouth, and there was a lovely smile on his face. He knew everything was going to be all right; everybody had made friends.

"Oh, dear me!" said Mrs Temperton trying to stifle her laughter. "You are a funny lot. Let's go inside, and you can tell us all about it."

Entering the cottage, Mrs Hardie's face lit up once

more.

"Oh my goodness! You've even changed my rooms around. What ever is next?"

Mrs McCue sat on the sofa next to Mrs Temperton and asked,"Who's going to believe all this?"

Mrs Temperton looked at Mustafa and said, "We won't tell anybody. We'll keep it our little secret."

Mrs Hardie came in with yet another tray of tea and put it on the coffee table, which had been moved into a corner.

"Come on everyone. Sit down where you can. I can't wait to hear your story," she commanded.

All the gnomes took their places in the centre of the floor, Mrs Temperton and Mrs McCue sat on the sofa, and Mrs Hardie sat in her favourite armchair.

Mustafa rose to his feet, and standing proudly in the centre of the room, started to tell his story – how he was a little lonely gnome who sat in the garden centre until he was bought by the Tempertons, taken home, and made to feel welcome and part of their family. He told them how the spark from the barbecue hit the remote star, which was now known to the gnomes as the Star of Life, and how it changed his tiny little world and the lives of all the garden ornaments in the village. He told them how it had changed Rufus and Dwain as well and how they kept an eye on the village when everybody was asleep.

"It's hard to believe, but I think I understand," remarked Mrs Hardie. "But why did you do all this for me?"

"He'll come to that in a moment," Lofty said, butting in. Glad for the moment of rest, Mustafa continued his story telling about the night the burglars arrived at the Temperton's house and how they chased them away, with Jester losing his float and getting soaking wet in the process and Timmy cracking his shell.

"I could go on for hours telling you what has happened in the village, but I think you want me to get to the point about the garden," Mustafa said.

The weather outside was beginning to clear. The dark, heavy clouds were dispersing, letting what sunlight there was creep through.

"Come on Jack," shouted Mr Temperton, walking out into his garden. "We haven't got much time left. I think the judges could be coming round about 6 o'clock. You can't do anything with the lawn; it's too wet, but just check that everything else is in the right place, with no dead leaves hanging off the tree."

All the men in the village were doing the same, spending the last few hours in their gardens, which they felt very proud of after all their hard work. At that moment, they didn't know what had happened to Mrs Hardie's garden or that she had entered the competition.

Back in the cottage, Mustafa was in full flow and had the full attention of everybody.

"Mrs Temperton, do you remember your neighbour coming round? You sat outside talking for about an hour," he continued. "Well, Lofty heard everything. He usually stands in your back garden holding onto a wheelbarrow."

"Yes, I remember," replied Mrs Temperton.

"He heard everything about a lonely, little old lady living across the road, who desperately wanted to enter the competition, but couldn't do it herself. Well, we thought that if we could help her, it would also help all of us by bonding us together. So, we set out to do the makeover. We didn't know what theme to use at first, but everything fell into place. We all really enjoyed doing it, and we are pleased with everyone's reaction. We hope that we haven't upset anyone. We only wanted to help."

"You've certainly done that. I'm very grateful for what you've done for me," Mrs Hardie told him, sipping another cup of tea very slowly. "What do we do now?"

Mrs McCue put down her cup and said, "First of all, you ought to ring the vicar. He's the chairman of the judges. Otherwise, he won't know you've entered the competition."

"I did. He was the first person I tried to contact this morning. There was no reply, but I left a message on his answering machine, saying that my garden was lovely and that I would enter the competition," Mrs Hardie told her.

The only thing that the Gnomes of Genom could do now was listen to what was being said and nod their little heads in agreement.

"Jack where are you?" shouted Mr Temperton in a worried voice. "Mustafa and all his friends have vanished. There's no fisherman by the pond, and the one whose arm was broken has gone too. I hope nobody's kidnapped them. I've read about that sort of thing in the newspapers."

"I'll go and have a look round and see if I can find them," Jack offered.

"What are we going to do?" shouted Mr Temperton. "Start near the stream."

Back in the cottage, Mrs Temperton stood up and said, "Why don't we just keep quiet and see who wins; then we can decide what to do."

Final Showdown

Mustafa and all his friends had made their way back to their own gardens as discreetly as possible, not knowing that Mr Temperton and Jack were out looking for them.

They arrived safely and returned to their normal positions, sitting there as though nothing had happened – the twins under the mushroom, Lofty in the middle of the lawn with his wheelbarrow, Timmy between the mushroom, and Jester who was sitting by his pond. Mustafa and Raymond took up their positions overlooking the whole of the garden from their little corner. All were feeling proud that they had achieved their goal.

The three ladies just sat in amazement looking at each other. They hadn't believed the makeover of the garden, until they saw it for themselves; however, talking gnomes and a talking dog take some believing, especially when they found out that the gnomes had worked so hard to please Mrs Hardie.

"I don't believe it," said Mrs Temperton. "Are we all dreaming? Just pinch me and tell me it's true."

"I feel numb as well," replied Mrs McCue. "It *must* be happening. We can't be dreaming!"

"I think it's lovely. Nobody'll believe us when we tell them. What a story! But one good thing is that we have the proof. Just look at my garden!" said Mrs Hardie, straightening herself in her chair. "Why don't we just walk through the village? Don't say anything to anybody. Let's see what happens."

For the rest of the morning, activity in the village took on a sense of urgency.

Everybody was rushing round putting the final touches on their gardens.

People at the far end of the village were still painting their garden fences. One or two were cleaning the cars standing in the driveways. Women were cleaning their windows, and even the children were getting involved by brushing the paths. Not a single thing had been overlooked.

Everything in the village shined and sparkled. Even the postman on his rounds had an extra bag with him, just in case any litter was still being blown around.

The time just flew by. People didn't have time to stand around chatting. Except, that is, for the three ladies – Mrs. Hardie, Mrs McCue and Mrs Temperton – who were just strolling around the village with smug little smiles on their faces, as though to say, "We know something that you don't!"

The three ladies walked the full length of the village, right down past the Genom Green Hotel, which looked magnificent covered in mottled green ivy, as far as the gates of Green End Farm.

"I must say I've never seen the village looking so lovely," remarked Mrs Temperton.

Mrs McCue nodded her head in agreement and suggested, "Let's go back to the hotel for afternoon tea. It's not every day that we have a chance to go out for a chat, and we have a lot of things to catch up on, thanks to Mrs Hardie."

"All right, but we must keep an eye on the time. I don't want to miss the judges," said Mrs Hardie, "and it really *is* nice to meet new friends."

* * * * * * *

"Jack" shouted Mr Temperton, running down the front path towards the road. "Where did you find them?"

"Find them? I haven't seen them," answered Jack.

"Well, they're all back in the garden, looking as though they've never moved," retorted Mr Temperton. "Somebody must be playing a joke on us."

"I'm not too sure," Jack said thoughtfully. "A lot of funny things have happened since we bought Mustafa and found all those other ones hidden under that pile of grass. I don't know what it is, but something strange is going on. Anyway, at least they are back just in time for the judging."

It was 6 o'clock, and everybody was waiting anxiously for the judges to knock on their front doors. There were five judges altogether: two men, two women, and the chairman of the judges, the Reverend Alf Johnson. They all came from the neighbouring village, which was called Beverlac because the beavers made their home in the stream, which also runs through Genom village.

First of all, they walked slowly around the village, looked at every house from a distance, and made notes of which ones had entered the competition. All the entrants had a yellow card in the front window.

The residents could be seen peeping through their net curtains, watching the judges' every move, and waiting for that knock on the door. Raymond the rabbit, Mustafa, and Timmy the tortoise positioned themselves by the gates of the Temperton's house while watching the judges coming closer.

"Are you sure they are the judges?" Timmy asked.

"They must be," answered Raymond. "I've never seen any of them before, and they do look very official, with all those papers in their hands."

"Step back a bit. Hide behind the railings of the gates so that they can't see us," Mustafa said.

"Look! That man has got his shirt on back to front," Timmy pointed at Reverend Johnson, laughing out of the side of his mouth. "And that other one looks as though he hasn't had his hair cut for at least two years." He continued his commentary, "I think one must be the vicar. The other man must be the local mayor. He looks quite official, especially with that chain round his neck."

Meanwhile, Raymond suggested to Mustafa that if all the gnomes spread themselves around Mrs Hardie's garden, it might make a big difference, especially with the French gnome, Pierre, and his Spanish friend, Juan, already there.

"After the judges have gone, we can rush back to our own gardens," he added.

"Not a bad idea Raymond," replied Mustafa. "Go and tell them all."

"Just look at those ladies! They have flowers stuck all over their dresses. I bet they made them themselves. They just seem to hang off them, no style whatsoever!" Mustafa said, his sense of fashion outraged. "Shush! They're heading this way."

Raymond whispered, "The lady in the matching skirt and jacket must be the mayor's wife, because she has a chain round her neck too. The other one just looks like a typical school teacher, with her glasses resting on the end of her nose."

"Never mind. Keep quiet! We don't want to be spotted," Mustafa shushed him.

Raymond was gone in a flash to tell all the gnomes to

go straight to Mrs Hardie's and take up their positions.

They rushed as fast as they could without being seen and took up their positions as Raymond had ordered.

There was Juan in the Spanish sector, standing on the sand. Pierre was near the big tower that he had made. Jester rushed in and sat as he normally did near the garden pond. Sam and Ella went and sat near Dwain the train. Willy and his friends were up in the Scottish highland garden, dressed neatly in their kilts. Plank and Simon were amongst the flowers.

Raymond, now feeling in control, stood on the back door step of Mrs Hardie's house and shouted down to the bottom of the garden.

"Can you all hear me? After the judges have gone, I want you all to rush very quietly back to your own gardens, without being seen, and do the same there."

The judges stopped outside the Temperton's house and formed a circle to discuss where to start.

"I think we have a difficult job on our hands," said Reverend Johnson. "The village itself looks very clean and tidy."

"I would call it very picturesque," remarked the lady judge with the glasses.

All the villagers were peering from behind their curtains watching the judges' every move with excitement and anticipation.

"We'll start up at the top. It looks like that cottage over there first," said the vicar, pointing to Mrs Hardie's house. "We'll walk round every garden with a yellow sticker in the window. I want you to judge everything relating to the gardens – colour, layout, tidiness, and most of all the overall aspect of the work involved. We'll work our way through the village and stop at the hotel to discuss our results over a drink. You all have a list of the entrants, so please make notes as you go around."

"Timmy! They're starting; you ought to make your way to the back garden. Try and be as quick as you can," ordered Mustafa in a nervous voice.

Mrs Hardie, Mrs McCue, and Mrs Temperton enjoyed their time together in the hotel and were now back home. Mrs Temperton tried to keep away from her husband. She knew how much this competition meant to him, and she didn't dare mention what had happened to Mrs Hardie.

Mrs McCue did the same, trying to keep in the kitchen out of the way.

Their husbands were both looking out of their windows, waiting nervously for that knock on the door.

Mrs Hardie was sitting in her favourite chair, without a care in the world. She was just thankful for what Mustafa and his friends had done for her. Winning the competition didn't really mean anything to her, but at least she had entered, and she was pleased she had taken part for the sake of the village.

There was the knock that everybody else had been dreading on Mrs Hardie's door.

Rufus got up off his mat by the back door, rushed out into the garden round to the front of the cottage, and barked as he went.

"Oh! Good evening, vicar," Mrs Hardie said as she answered the door. "Come on through."

"No, we won't, thank you. We'll go round the side if that's all right. Our shoes are already dirty. We just wanted permission to enter your garden," said the vicar, with Rufus sniffing at his shoes.

"Don't worry about him," said Mrs Hardie picking up Rufus who was now wagging his tail. "He's just pleased to see you. Help yourselves. Just go round the corner. I'll meet you at the back." Mrs Hardie had a contented smile on her face.

All the gnomes were in position, standing proud, in their green hats and neat clothes – except of course for Button, who seemed to have put on weight, as his jacket stretched further across his stomach.

Rufus sat by the back door, scared in case someone talked to him and he talked back without thinking. He had done it once. He dare not do it again.

The group of judges took their time walking around looking at everything, not saying a word, just making the odd note on their papers. The mayor and his wife spent a lot of time looking at Dwain in his tunnel with Willy in the background.

After about fifteen minutes, the vicar returned to Mrs Hardie and thanked her for all the effort that she had obviously put into the garden.

Mrs Hardie smiled, "No problem. I've thoroughly enjoyed doing it. Do you like it?"

"I'm afraid we can't comment at this stage, but I will say you've done an excellent job. If all the gardens are like this, we have a hard task."

Taking their leave, the mayoress turned to Mrs Hardie and said, "I hope we'll see you tomorrow when we give out the results."

"I wouldn't miss it for the world," Mrs Hardie replied with a big smile on her face.

"Right lads, they've gone!" shouted Rufus from the doorstep. "Off you go and thanks for everything."

The gnomes all sneaked off as quietly as possible, while the five judges stood outside Mrs Hardie's cottage, checking where to go next.

"Number 40 is next. It's just across the road over there," said the vicar pointing to Mr and Mrs McCue's house.

Willy and his friends were out of breath having dashed across the road, but made it just in time, before the judges entered the garden accompanied by Mr and Mrs McCue.

Mrs McCue stood in the background, watching her husband point out all the main features of his hard work, hoping that the judges would appreciate his efforts.

Mr Temperton, who lived next door, saw the judges enter the McCue's drive and knew he must be next. He was very anxious and started pacing up and down while glancing out of the window every so often. He didn't know what to do with himself.

"Oh sit down, dear; you've done all you can. It's up to the judges. Nothing you do now will make any difference," remarked Mrs Temperton.

"I know but Jack and I have worked so hard on the garden. I really would like to win," he told her.

"You'll still have to wait until tomorrow," smiled Mrs Temperton.

Suddenly that dreaded knock rattled the front door.

Mr Temperton was frozen to the floor. He couldn't move and was shaking all over.

"Come on, dear. Go and answer the door. You know who it is. The time has come," Mrs Temperton said firmly.

Having to think how to put one foot in front of the other, he slowly made his way to the door.

"Good evening," he greeted the judges. "I presume you

have come to look at my garden. Would you like to make your way round the back?"

Without a thought in his head, Mr Temperton closed the door and rushed through the house to arrive in the garden before the judges.

"Where would you like to start?" he asked the vicar.

"We'll just wander around if that's all right with you. Why don't you just sit there," suggested the vicar pointing to the chair under the kitchen window as the five judges started to move round the garden.

Sam spoke to Ella out of the side of his mouth, "Put a smile on your face! This it it!"

Timmy mumbled to Jester, who was sitting at the side of the pond and could see everything that was going on, "They're coming!"

Lofty's legs began to shake. He had never felt so nervous, and his wheelbarrow felt heavier than ever.

Mustafa sat proudly in his position, eyeing everything

that was going on around him. He noticed Mrs Temperton looking out of the kitchen window. She gave him a little wave and a reassuring smile.

Mustafa didn't dare wave back, but his thoughts took him back to when he was in the garden centre, picked up by the Tempertons, brought home, and then made many new friends through the Star of Life from the barbeque.

"Yes, I am Mustafa. Yes, my friends are happy. I am *very* happy."

The judges took their time, checking everything, even the size of the fruit on the pomegranate tree.

Jack arrived by the side of the house. "Am I too late?"

"I think they're just finishing," Mr Temperton told him. "They've spent longer looking around than I thought."

The lady judge, whose dress was covered in flowers, made her way to Mr Temperton, and said, "I must say, you have a lovely garden. You must be proud of it."

This time, it was Raymond who looked at Mustafa

with a smile.

"Thank you very much. We'll announce the winner tomorrow," said the vicar, as they made their way round the corner of the house checking their papers to see where to go next.

Mrs Temperton appeared at the back door, turned to her husband and Jack who were sitting on the bench, and said, "Well, that's that!"

Rufus scampered into the garden and went straight up to Timmy, who was half hidden by some grass. "How did it go?" he asked.

Timmy replied, "OK, I think. They didn't say much. We'll all have to wait."

The judges walked down the main street. One of them stopped and said, "We'll have to be quicker. It's a quarter past seven already, and we've only seen three gardens. We could still be wandering around at midnight at this rate."

"We do have a job to do, and it's important to the

contestants. We'll spend as much time as is necessary," the vicar insisted.

Mrs McCue walked round to her neighbour's house, passing Mr Temperton and Jack.

"Is your wife in?" she asked.

"Yes, she's in the kitchen," came the reply. Mrs McCue went into the house.

"How did it go?" Mrs McCue asked in a quizzing voice.

"Come on! Let's go outside and walk round the garden. I don't want my husband to hear anything." Mrs Temperton grabbed Mrs McCue by the arm.

They made their way towards the pond, knowing that whatever they said would be heard by Mustafa and his friends.

"I've been sitting at home thinking while the judges came round," Mrs McCue said, making sure that the gnomes could hear her. "This day has changed all our lives, thanks to our little friends here. Wouldn't it be nice if we could get them all to sit round the Village Green tomorrow when we get the results?"

Raymond was gone in a flash. This time he hadn't waited for Mustafa's approval, but he didn't care. He knew straight away it would be a nice gesture to be there for the results.

"What a long and interesting day it's been," remarked Mrs Temperton. "Nobody's going to believe any of what's happened in this village today."

The judging continued late into the night until finally the judges arrived exhausted at the hotel.

They placed their order with the barman and sat in a dark corner of the lounge to finalise their decision.

The Village Garden Fete

Today is the day of the Village Garden Fete, when all the villagers rally round and join in together to have a bit of fun. The results of the Garden Competition also are to be announced.

The weather has been kind, the sun is breaking through, and only a few fluffy clouds remain in the sky.

The Gnomes of Genom have a funny feeling of excitement in their tummies. They know that all their hard work in the village will be rewarded in some way, even if someone else takes the praise. (As long as their work has been recognised, they will be happy.)

Raymond the rabbit spent most of last night going round to all his friends in the village. He asked them to make their way to the Village Green very early in the morning and take up positions around the green, so that when people arrived to set up their stalls, they would think somebody else put them there.

Mrs Hardie, the little old lady who lived in the cottage, got up at her usual time and looked out of her window to see if her garden was still the same. Nothing had altered. However, she noticed that Dwain the train wasn't in his tunnel, and Juan and Pierre were missing.

Turning and looking down at Rufus, her little faithful dog who was always by her side, she asked, "Rufie, what's going on?"

Rufus jumped up and put his front paws on her thigh, saying, "Everyone's gone to get ready for the fete. I think."

Mrs Hardie trotted across the road to ask Mrs McCue if she knew anything about it.

"Oh yes, it was my idea. I mentioned it to Mrs Temperton last night. I thought it would be nice if all our little gnome friends sat round the green."

"That's nice," Mrs Hardie replied.

With that, Mrs McCue decided to see if Willy was still siting with his friends in her garden. She peered through the window and smiled.

People were arriving at the Village Green to prepare their stalls, which included a cake stall, Tombola, a Bring-and-Buy stall, local-grown produce, and many stalls just for fun, like throw the ping-pong ball into a bucket and hoopla.

You could hear people enquiring, "Where have all these gnomes come from? I haven't seen so many in one place before."

Mr Temperton stepped out into his garden, carrying a mug of tea, and started walking towards his shed. He paused in the middle of the lawn and spun around with a frantic look on his face.

"Oh my word, it's happened again," he says in a loud voice.

He ran back towards the house shouting as loud as he could trying to catch his wife's attention.

"What's the matter with you?" Mrs Temperton enquired.

"All our gnomes have vanished again. I didn't notice at first, until I stopped in the middle of the lawn where the wheelbarrow should be and looked towards the pond, and that one has gone as well," Mr Temperton continued, trying to get his breath.

"The mushroom's still here, but nothing else; the same thing happened last night, just before the judges came round."

"Are you sure it isn't a dream." Mrs Temperton asked, knowing where they had gone.

"No, just look for yourself," said her husband still dazed.

Mrs Temperton tried to calm him down, using any excuse she could and hoping that he did not go to the centre of the village.

"What's going to happen if I win the competition and people want to come and have a look at what we've done? It will be embarrassing."

"Don't worry dear. Just calm down," she said. "Everything will be all right."

Except for Jester and Willy, Mustafa and all his friends arrived at the village green, just before the sun started to rise, through the light mist. Jester and Willy felt that they had to have a go on the slide in the park just for fun; they felt as though they deserved a break after all the hard work they had done over the past few days.

Mustafa was astonished by the number of gnomes already seated around the Village Green when he arrived.

"Raymond, where have all these gnomes come from? I've never seen them before. There must be at least 25 of them," Mustafa said in a stern voice.

"I didn't want to tell you, but as the people started doing their gardens, they found more and more gnomes hidden under piles of wood, grass, and even in their garages. They all have the Genom green hat on, the same as you, so they must have been affected at the same time when the spark struck our Star of Life," Raymond replied.

"Do they know about the three ladies who can understand us?" Mustafa asked.

"No, I haven't told them that or what we have been doing. I just asked them to be here this morning," Raymond replied with a sorry expression on his face.

Luckily, none of the stall holders had arrived, so Mustafa waddled over to them and introduced himself as their leader. He explained what they had been doing and how the colours of their hats had changed and why.

"Please don't talk when you are standing here, as we have found out that three ladies in the village can understand every word we say. We have only spoken to them, so we do not know if everybody else can understand," remarked

Mustafa.

They all agreed to keep the secret, as long as Mustafa promised to tell them everything later.

Mrs McCue and Mrs Hardie made cakes for the stall and decided to walk down through the village and give them to the ladies who were preparing the stall. It was really an excuse to see if all the gnomes had gathered round the green.

As soon as they were in sight of the green, they turned to each other, smiled, and very carefully put an arm round each other, whilst holding onto their cakes in their other hands.

"It's worked," Mrs McCue laughed. "Oh don't they look magnificent? How are we ever going to thank them for what they have done?"

"We'll find a way; I'm sure of that," Mrs Hardie remarked.

The fete was about to start, and people were beginning to arrive. They were chatting as they walked around; many of them had brought local vegetables and plants that they had grown in their own gardens, such as potatoes, carrots, lettuce, and colourful plants.

"The cake stall appears to be the busiest," remarked Ella.

"Shush, we are not supposed to be talking," Sam said, squeezing her hand.

Mr and Mrs Temperton walked slowly through the village towards the fete. Mr Temperton was trying to glance through many of the fences to see if he could spot any of his missing gnomes.

"Oh stop it dear; you'll find out soon enough," smiled Mrs Temperton.

After getting closer and closer to all the activity taking place, Mr Temperton stopped and rubbed his eyes. "Look, look; they are all here. How on earth did they get here?"

"Oh shut up for once, and do as you are told," snarled Mrs Temperton.

A long table stood in the centre of the green; it was covered with a blue cloth with three silver cups, which were all different sizes, placed in the middle.

Laughing and giggling could be heard amongst the continuous chatter as all the villagers began to gather round the table.

"I just can't believe it," Mr Temperton said. "Look how many gnomes are here."

Mrs McCue was stopped by the lady who ran the post office.

"This is lovely. Look at all the gnomes. Don't they make a nice change? It just seems to add that little bit of difference. Do you know where they all came from?" she asked.

"Everybody is asking me the same thing, but I haven't got a clue," Mrs McCue replied, making her way to speak to her neighbours.

Tap, tap. "Can everybody hear me?"

A voice suddenly appeared from nowhere. "Ladies and Gentlemen, may I welcome you to the Genom Village Fete."

People noticed that the vicar had arrived at the table in the centre, speaking into a microphone, which seemed to echo for miles.

"Before we announce the winners of the garden competition, I would just like to say that it has been a very hard decision. You all must have worked very hard, as the standard was exceptional, but we can only choose the best three. So, I would like to ask the mayor to present the trophies."

The mayor walked towards the microphone, saying, "Thank you vicar." Raising his voice, he continued. "I agree with every word he has just said. I have never seen gardens that carry so much colour, and the planning of them must have taken more time than the actual digging and mowing of the lawns."

"I am sure you would like me to thank the team of judges for their time and the organisers for arranging this event."

Everybody started clapping in appreciation.

The mayor cleared his throat with a loud cough.

"In third place with a total of 155 points. Mr and Mrs McCue."

A small rapture of applause was heard as Mrs McCue stepped forward to collect the smallest of the three silver cups, which was handed to her by the mayoress.

"In second place…"

Mr Temperton began to shake; he was hoping that it wouldn't be him. He wanted to win.

"In second place, with a total of 160 points is…"

Mr Temperton held his wife's hand and looked down at

his feet; he couldn't bear to look at the mayor.

"Mr Temperton."

Suddenly, all the air in his lungs had gone; he gasped for some more. His wife gave him a kiss on the cheek saying, "Well done dear."

He walked gingerly towards the mayoress, put his acceptance speech back into his pocket, kissed her on the cheek, accepted the silver trophy, and stood next to Mrs McCue.

"The winner's of this year's garden competition had a very high standard in all respects, so with a total of 175 points the winner is…"

Silence surrounded the village.

"Mrs Hardie."

Suddenly, Dwain could not hold back his excitement and gave three hoots on his whistle, which was followed by all the gnomes jumping and waving their hats in the air, shouting, "We've done it!"

Everybody turned round looking puzzled at all the excited gnomes waving their arms in the air.

"Pinch me. I don't believe what I am seeing," Mr Temperton said.

Mrs Temperton and Mrs McCue were also jumping up and down with excitement and hugging Mrs Hardie, who couldn't really believe it.

The crowd began to applaud again, as Mrs Hardie walked forward to collect her prize from the mayor; she exchanged kisses and with a firm handshake accepted the trophy and the title of the best-kept garden in Genom.

"Please say a few words," said the vicar butting in.

Feeling a bit embarrassed, Mrs Hardie picked up the microphone. "Ladies and Gentlemen," she paused in thought. "No that's not right. Friends sounds better. I can only accept this honour with the help that I have received from all my little friends that you see spread around the green."

Dwain gave another whistle.

"I woke up one morning, and my garden was beautiful, thanks to Mustafa and friends," she continued.

"Mustafa," said Mr Temperton to his wife. "He belongs to us, doesn't he?"

"I don't think so anymore; he's the pride of Genom."

"My little friends found out that I wanted to take part in the competition, so they decided to help me by doing a makeover. Anyway, it's a long story, but I would just like to say that I couldn't have done it without them, and now they are part of my life. We can understand each other."

"And me, don't forget me," Rufus said, wagging his tail by her feet.

Mrs Hardie placed the cup back on the table, bent down and picked Rufus up, and gave him a big hug. He responded by licking her face all over.

"Thank you very much everybody," said Mrs Hardie walking back into the crowd.

Mr Temperton had now accepted defeat gracefully, with the knowledge that it was his gnome that won the prize, with the help of his friends.

He walked up to Mustafa and bent forward with his hand extended. Mustafa responded by shaking his hand.

"I had this funny feeling something was going on behind my back, when you all went missing the other day and when your hats changed colour. Anyway, welcome to the village."

Mustafa felt very humble, receiving the congratulations from his owner.

All the people at the fete were talking in disbelief as to what they had just heard. They heard another tap on the microphone.

"Hello, hello can you hear me? I've never used one of these before."

Everybody turned towards the table again, only to see Mustafa and Raymond standing on top of the table.

Mustafa cleared his throat, just the same as the mayor, in case it was the done thing.

"If I may say something, please don't be afraid of all my friends; thanks to a spark from Mr Temperton's barbeque and a thunder storm, we came to life. We are here to help you in any way we can, and I believe that it is only my friends and the villagers that can understand each other."

Mustafa coughed again.

"Please try and get to know us. Every one of us has our own stories to tell."

Printed in the United Kingdom by
Lightning Source UK Ltd., Milton Keynes
137663UK00002B/24/P

9 781438 957890